'Rafferty—'

'They're going to

He was all business

'Then we'll just have to climb the last few feet to reach the crew.'

The ground looked an awfully long way away from where they were standing, and she gulped at the thought of dangling off a thin little cable while she lowered herself down the mountainside.

'You'll be fine.' Rafferty pulled her to him and hugged her hard, and she heard the sudden roughness in his voice. 'I won't let anything bad happen to you, Natalie.'

Emotion welled up inside her so that it was hard to smile back at him when she felt so choked up. 'I know you won't,' she said huskily.

'Do you?'

The urgency in his voice was impossible to ignore. 'I would trust you with my life,' she said simply. Because it was true.

Dear Reader

I have always been fascinated by the work that is carried out by overseas aid agencies, and really admire the courage and dedication of the brave doctors and nurses who volunteer to help other people under the most arduous conditions. Setting up my own fictional medical aid agency is my tribute to them.

I knew as soon as I introduced Natalie and Rafferty in the first book of my **Worlds Together** series that I would have to tell their story! That's how it happens sometimes—characters suddenly appear on a page, bringing with them their own issues.

Natalie and Rafferty are both strong-minded people who love one another, but they cannot get past the fact that Natalie is immensely wealthy and Rafferty isn't. It sounds so simple put like that, but it's Natalie's wealth which is keeping them apart. Although Rafferty is a top-flight surgeon, and highly respected in his field, he isn't sure if he can live up to Natalie's expectations.

Helping these two people resolve their problems was a fascinating process. They skirt around each other, argue frequently and dig in their heels before they finally admit they are both at fault. Even I breathed a huge sigh of relief when they eventually realised that they couldn't live without one another!

It's the most wonderful feeling when you know that you have given your characters the story they deserve. That's how I felt at the end of NURSE IN A MILLION, and I hope you will too.

Best wishes

Jennifer

You can visit my website at: www.jennifer-taylor.com

NURSE IN A MILLION

BY
JENNIFER TAYLOR

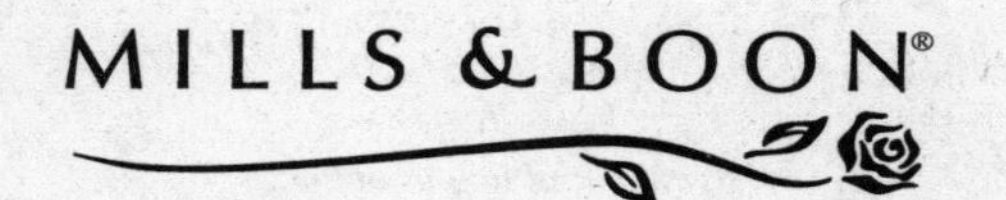

First published in Great Britain 2005
Harlequin Mills & Boon Limited,
Eton House, 18-24 Paradise Road, Richmond, Surrey TW9 1SR

ISBN 0 263 84341 6

Set in Times Roman 10¼ on 11½ pt.
03-1105-57520

Printed and bound in Spain
by Litografia Rosés, S.A., Barcelona

PROLOGUE

'INCOMING wounded. Stand clear!'

Michael James Rafferty sighed as he tossed the paper towel he'd been using into the waste sack. He'd been in Theatre since five that morning and he was far too tired to appreciate all these stupid games. Snapping on a fresh pair of gloves, he turned to the newcomer.

'We're not starring in an episode of *M.A.S.H.* here, Sandy, so just tell me what's wrong with the patient and leave out the rest.'

'Oh, um, yes, right. Sorry.'

The younger man looked abashed as he wheeled the trolley into the tent and Rafferty sighed again. It was Sandy Baxendale's first mission with Worlds Together, a leading international medical aid agency, so it was little wonder that he tended to get carried away by the drama of it all. Rafferty made a note not to be too hard on him in future but with over two dozen missions to his credit, he found it difficult to remember when he'd felt the same kind of excitement. Oh, there was still a certain satisfaction when he managed to save a life under the most arduous conditions, but there was no longer that buzz to the job there'd been once upon a time.

Maybe it was the fact that Natalie was no longer working with them that had made all the difference, he mused, then blanked out the thought. There was no point going down that route again.

'OK, so what have we got?' He ran a critical eye over the young woman on the trolley. 'A bit of a mess, isn't she? Where was she found?'

'One of the search-and-rescue teams found her buried under the remains of the maternity unit,' Sandy explained. 'They've no idea if she's a patient or a member of the staff.'

'Did they find anyone else there alive?' Rafferty asked as he started to examine her. He gently palpated her abdomen but there were no obvious signs that she'd given birth in the days preceding the mudslide which had engulfed a large area of Guatemala. The Worlds Together team had flown out to the region as soon as the Guatemalan government had declared it a national disaster. That had been four days ago and he knew the chances of them finding many more survivors were decreasing by the hour.

'Two babies. They were still in their cots and that's probably what saved their lives, according to the search-and-rescue guys. They think the cots must have floated when the mud started to fill up the nursery.' Sandy shook his head in amazement. 'It's incredible that anyone survived when you see the state of the place. The whole area has been literally swamped by mud.'

'It's been a bad incident,' Rafferty agreed, gently feeling his way down the girl's body and adding a fractured pelvis to the growing list of her injuries.

'It's far worse than I imagined it would be,' the young male nurse admitted. 'I know we were told to expect the worst but I was really shocked when I saw the extent of the damage.'

'It's always hard to take it all in,' Rafferty said soberly. 'That's why some people find it difficult to cope with this type of work. We lose a lot of new recruits because they can't handle the sheer scale of a disaster like this.'

'Oh, I can handle it all right,' Sandy hastily assured him. 'It just took a day or so to get my head round it all. Even in the busiest accident-and-emergency department, you don't get such a concentration of severely injured as we've dealt with here.'

Rafferty nodded as he moved around the trolley. A fractured ankle was duly noted this time. 'It's the same for all of us, if it's any consolation.'

'Really?' Sandy exclaimed. 'You mean that you still find it a bit overwhelming at times?'

'Yes. You certainly shouldn't let yourself become blasé about the job because that's when you could find yourself in real trouble.'

'That's what Miss Palmer said at my interview. She told me that the minute you feel as though it's just routine is the time you should stop.' The younger man frowned. 'I wasn't sure what she meant but I think I understand now. You can't afford to grow complacent because you might forget about the dangers.'

'That's right,' Rafferty said shortly because this second reminder of Natalie, coming on top of the other, had pushed a few internal buttons. He breathed deeply to quell feelings that had been lying dormant for some time. It really wasn't the right moment to start thinking about how much he missed her.

'Right, we'll take her straight to Theatre and do the X-rays there,' he said briskly. 'There's bound to be extensive soft-tissue damage and I don't want to waste any time. Can you tell Ben that I'll need him to do the anaesthetic, and let Patsy know that I'd like her to assist me.'

'Patsy was in Theatre all last night,' Sandy told him. 'She's trying to catch up on her sleep so do you want me to wake her up?'

Rafferty frowned. 'Better not. What about Lauren?'

'She's in Theatre Two with Liam. I'm not sure how long they'll be yet.'

'Then it looks like it's you and me. I know you don't have a lot of experience in Theatre so do you think you can cope?'

'Of course,' Sandy assured him, but Rafferty could tell that he wasn't nearly as confident as he was pretending to be.

'OK. Scrub up once you've told Ben that I need him.'

He didn't say anything else because it would serve no purpose to undermine Sandy's confidence. However, it was worrying to have to rely on staff who lacked the necessary skills. He quickly unzipped the flap and let himself into the scrub area. Each of the theatre tents was really three tents set one inside the other. The first section was where the patients were examined, the second was the scrub area and the third and final section was the actual operating theatre.

Conditions in there were kept sterile thanks to an expensive air-filtration system bought for them by their main sponsor, Palmer Pharmaceuticals. Palmer's had also paid for the state-of-the-art operating tables and the high-tech lighting equipment that ran off generators. If it weren't for the company's generosity, Rafferty knew that Worlds Together wouldn't be able to carry out its work so effectively. Palmer's provided most of the money they needed, and that was what lay at the heart of his own problems.

Natalie Palmer, the woman he loved more than life itself, was heiress to the Palmer fortune. Was it any wonder their relationship had faltered?

Three hours later, Rafferty left Theatre. Tossing his gown into a sack, he went straight outside. It was just gone six and the camp was quiet for once. The rest of the team were having dinner and he knew he should join them but he wasn't hungry. Although he'd done all he could, he hadn't been able to save the girl and her loss weighed heavily on him.

'I'm really sorry. I did my best but I just wasn't up to the job.'

He looked round when Sandy followed him outside. The young nurse's lack of experience had been very apparent and several times Rafferty had had to tell him what to do. It hadn't been an ideal situation, by any means, but it hadn't been Sandy's fault the girl had died and Rafferty took immediate steps to tell him that.

He sighed as he watched the younger man heading towards the mess tent a short time later. His pep talk might have had the desired effect but it wasn't right that people should start blaming themselves because they lacked the necessary skills. Ever since Natalie had left the team, they'd had problems finding a suitable replacement and it was galling to know that she was wasting her talents, sitting behind a desk in London. She was a nurse, not a businesswoman, for heaven's sake!

Rafferty's expression was grim as he swung round and strode across the compound. It was high time that someone told her that.

CHAPTER ONE

'I'M VERY sorry, Miss Palmer, but he's still refusing to leave. He's been here for over an hour now and I really don't know what else I can do.'

Natalie Palmer sighed when she heard the panic in her secretary's voice. Janet was noted for her calm efficiency but even she was starting to crack under the pressure. 'Did you explain that I was too busy to see anyone this morning without an appointment?'

'Yes! But he said that he was prepared to wait all day if necessary.' Janet lowered her voice so that Natalie had to strain her ears to hear what she was saying. 'Would you like me to call Security and let them deal with him?'

It was tempting.

Very tempting, indeed!

Natalie hesitated as she weighed up the merits of having Dr Michael James Rafferty ejected from the headquarters of Palmer Pharmaceuticals. After all, why should she worry about the embarrassment it might cause him? Rafferty obviously didn't care that he was making a spectacle of himself, otherwise he would have left as soon as she'd made it clear that she didn't intend to see him. No, the truth was that Rafferty was too stubborn to accept that he wasn't going to get his own way.

Her mouth thinned, because in her opinion Rafferty's stubbornness was the cause of all their problems. After all, it wasn't *her* fault that her family was so rich. If it didn't worry her then she didn't see why it should worry him. But he wouldn't accept that her wealth didn't matter so long as they loved one another. If he'd been the sort of person to suffer from low self-esteem, she could have understood, but Rafferty certainly wasn't lacking in confidence. Why should he, when he'd reached the very top of his profession and earned the respect of his peers along the way?

'Miss Palmer? Are you still there?'

'Yes. I'm sorry, Janet. I was just trying to decide what to do for the best.'

Natalie hurriedly returned her thoughts to her current predicament. If it needed drastic measures to resolve this problem, she wouldn't back down. Rafferty couldn't just turn up at her office and demand to see her—it gave out the completely wrong signals.

Since her father's heart attack three months ago, she had worked hard to keep Palmer Pharmaceuticals on track. Richard Palmer had warned her there were certain factions within the company who wanted to change how the firm operated. Palmer's had always donated a large percentage of its profits to charitable ventures and in recent years it had been the main sponsor of Worlds Together. It was a costly undertaking and Natalie knew that several members of the board would prefer to see the money spent elsewhere.

That was the last thing she intended to happen. As a highly skilled nurse-practitioner, she'd been involved with Worlds Together since its inception and knew how valuable its work was. She really wasn't prepared to jeopardise its future by allowing her authority to be undermined in any way.

'I think it would be best if you called Security,' she told Janet, trying not to think about how much she longed to see Rafferty. He'd made his position abundantly clear before she'd come back to London and she doubted if he'd changed his mind. 'Ask them to escort Dr Rafferty—'

She broke off when her office door suddenly opened and Rafferty appeared. He gave her a broad smile but she could see the glitter in his eyes, and a shiver ran through her because it was obvious that he hadn't appreciated being kept waiting.

'Hello, Natalie. How are you?'

'Get out!'

'Tut-tut, that isn't very polite, is it? And after I've spent so much time waiting to see you, too.' He glanced at his watch and arched a sleek dark brow. 'Over an hour. I am impressed. I didn't think you'd hold out that long, but it will teach me not to underestimate you in future, won't it, sweetheart?'

'I am not your sweetheart,' she told him, coldly enunciating every word.

'Not now, maybe, but you were once and it wasn't that long ago either.'

He closed the door and slid home the bolt, shaking his head when she immediately reached for the phone. 'If you're thinking of calling Security, I wouldn't bother. I'm sure your secretary will do it for you.'

Natalie slammed the receiver back into its cradle. 'Then why not spare yourself the embarrassment of being thrown out? There's the door, Rafferty. Make sure you close it again on your way out.'

'Cute. You've obviously been sharpening your tongue while I've been hanging around outside.'

He laughed as he crossed the room and Natalie felt her heart give a nervous little flutter. It was three months since she'd seen him and it struck her all over again just how handsome he was. With that crisp black hair, those deep green eyes and chiselled features, Rafferty could turn any woman's head and she certainly wasn't immune to his charms. However, she doubted if this was a social visit and didn't intend to make the mistake of falling under his spell again that day.

'My secretary has already explained that I'm extremely busy. I really don't have time for this, Rafferty, so if you want to see me then I suggest you make an appointment like everyone else does.'

'But I'm not ''everyone else'', am I?' He stopped in front of her desk and regarded her steadily. 'You and I go back a long way, Natalie, and I think that gives me certain rights.'

'What sort of rights?' she demanded scornfully.

'The right to tell one another the truth, for starters.'

He leant across the desk and she steeled herself when she saw how grim he looked all of a sudden. She had a feeling that she wasn't going to like what he had to say, but she couldn't think of a way to stop him.

'You've sold out, Natalie. You've swapped a career where you were doing an awful lot of good for one spent making money. Now, maybe you enjoy the cut and thrust of business and get a real buzz from it—I really don't know. But can you put your hand on your heart and swear that what you're doing now is anywhere near as fulfilling as nursing was?'

'I'm not listening to this,' she began, but he ignored her as he carried on.

'Of course you can't. And if you'd just admit that you were wrong to take on this job, you could come back to what you do best.'

'Wrong?'

'Yes!' There was a touch of impatience in his voice now. 'Oh, I'm sure you've done your best but you have to face facts, and fact number one is that you're not a businesswoman. There must be hundreds of people better qualified than you who could do this job.'

'You have no idea what *this job* entails!' she shot back, scarcely able to believe his arrogance. Just who did he think he was to decide that she wasn't making a success of running the company?

He shrugged, obviously unfazed by her anger. 'I know that it involves making a lot of money.'

'And that's all there is to it? Making money?' She tossed

back her head and laughed. 'You haven't a clue, Rafferty! You've no idea what goes into running this company because if you had, you might change your mind.'

'About the challenges entailed in making vast amounts of profit for its shareholders?' He smiled thinly. 'I don't think so. Somehow I don't think it would hold much appeal for me.'

'How do you know when you've never tried it?'

'I know that making money can never equate with saving lives. That's what you're trained to do, in case you've forgotten. You save people's lives. You care for them when they're sick and you make them better.'

He glanced around the beautifully appointed office with its stunning view over the River Thames and she could see the contempt on his face when he turned back to her. 'Can you honestly say that what you're doing now is more important than that? Because if you can, you're not the woman I thought you were.'

Natalie felt a stabbing pain pierce her heart. Was her worth only to be measured by the number of lives she saved? She pushed back her chair and stood up, unwilling to sit there and listen to anything else.

'You've said what you came to say and now I think you should leave.'

'I'm not leaving until I get a proper answer from you.'

'No, what you mean, Rafferty, is that you're not leaving until I agree with you. That's why you came, isn't it? Because you intended to…*bully* me into falling in with your wishes!'

'Bully you?'

He looked taken aback by the accusation but it was of little consolation. She couldn't believe how painful it was to know that he valued her more as a nurse than a woman. Even though they'd never been able to resolve their differences about her family's fortune, the one thought she'd clung to had been that it had proved he'd loved her for herself. Now even that was in doubt, it seemed.

'What else would you call it? Coming here and demanding that I admit I was wrong to help my father… That's typical bullying tactics in my eyes.'

'I didn't say that you were wrong to help your father.'

'No?' She laughed shortly, too hurt to take a rational view of events. 'It sounded like it to me, but maybe I'm wrong about that, too. We can't all be as perfect as you, Rafferty, unfortunately.'

'I'm far from perfect,' he ground out. 'I've made more mistakes in my life than I can count. That's why I can't bear to see you making a mistake like this. You shouldn't be here, Natalie. You should be doing the work you're trained to do, not playing the big executive in this fancy office.'

'I'm not playing, I assure you. I admit that I'm having to learn the job as I go along, and that I shall never be anywhere near as good at it as my father is. But I do my best and, despite what you believe, it makes a difference to people's lives, just in a different way.'

'By clinching deals and making money?' He laughed harshly. 'Not quite the cutting edge kind of work you're used to, but maybe you've forgotten what it's like to work at the sharp end. Maybe you need a reminder of what's really important in this life.'

'I don't need any reminders, thank you very much.'

'I disagree. It's obvious that somewhere during the past three months you've lost your way. The question now is whether you have the guts to do something about it.'

'What do you mean by that?'

'Prove that you know what you're doing by coming on our next aid mission. If you still feel that working here is more important after that then I swear that I'll never try to persuade you to change your mind again. Are you up to it, though, Natalie? That's the big question.'

Rafferty held his breath. Even though he'd never planned on issuing such a challenge when he'd set out that morning, he realised all of a sudden that it might be the only way to make her see sense. If he could get her back into the field, she'd soon realise what was important to her…

'Was that a challenge?'

Her tone was clipped and he winced at the supercilious note it held. It was unheard of for Natalie to speak to anyone that way. Despite her background, she had never put on airs and graces and had always treated everyone in the same friendly fashion. He must have really upset her to arouse such a response and it didn't make him feel good to know that. He had to console himself with the thought that he was doing this for her own benefit.

'If you prefer to see it as a challenge, it's fine by me.'

'And if I accept, what are you going to do in return?'

She walked around the desk and sat down on one of the low leather sofas in front of the window. Rafferty felt a wave of heat shoot through him as he watched her settle herself comfortably against the cushions. She was wearing a pale grey suit which he knew without needing to see the label must have come from some exclusive designer's collection. The jacket fitted her like a glove, moulding her full breasts and offering a tantalising glimpse of cleavage when she bent forward to help herself to a grape from the fruit bowl on the coffee-table. It was obvious that she wasn't wearing anything under the jacket apart from a bra and his body responded in time-honoured fashion to the knowledge.

'Why should I need to do anything?' he countered, hoping she couldn't tell what was happening to him.

'Because it's only fair, of course.'

She popped the grape into her mouth and crossed her legs. It was done with the utmost decorum but he had to stifle a groan when he heard the whisper of silk. Although most women didn't bother wearing stockings nowadays, Natalie had always preferred to wear them. In fact, they'd enjoyed many a happy hour divesting her of them…

'If I accept your challenge, you should accept mine. Unless you're too scared, of course.'

That got his immediate attention. Rafferty blanked out the delicious images that had been playing inside his head and stared at her. 'I'm not scared, Natalie. If the only way to make you see sense is by accepting your challenge, I'll do it.'

'Good. That's what I hoped you'd say.'

She stood up and came towards him, stopping so close that he could feel the warmth of her body all down the length of his. Trying to control his rioting libido at that point was a waste of time so he gave up. If she was deliberately trying to torment him, she was making a damn good job of it, he thought ruefully.

'I'll expect you tonight at six. Don't be late. It really isn't good form to arrive after the main guest. Oh, and you'll need a dinner jacket, too. I'd hate you to feel embarrassed by not being properly dressed.'

She swished past him before he could say anything, shot back the bolt and opened the door. A couple of burly security guards rushed into the room and grasped him by the arms. Rafferty tried to shake them off but soon realised that he was wasting his time. Anyway, he'd be damned if he'd give her the satisfaction of watching him struggle.

'Escort Dr Rafferty from the building and inform the staff on Reception that he isn't to be admitted again today.' She turned to Janet, who had followed the men into the room. 'Dr Rafferty will need a pass so can you make all the necessary arrangements, please? I'll sign the authorisation forms myself.'

'A pass?' the secretary repeated uncertainly, glancing at him.

Rafferty really couldn't blame her for being confused, because he was feeling a bit that way himself. He dug in his heels as the men tried to hustle him out of the room.

'What the hell is going on, Natalie? Why are you ordering a pass for me when you're having me thrown out?'

'Because you can't just come in here and throw your weight around. It really isn't on, Rafferty, and I'm not prepared to put up with it.' She smiled calmly at him as she went and sat down behind her desk. 'However, a pass is essential if you're to complete the challenge I've set you.'

'What challenge?' he demanded as the men hauled him through the open door. 'Natalie…!'

'That you spend a month in my world and see how well *you* cope.'

CHAPTER TWO

'LADIES and gentlemen, it gives me great pleasure to introduce our guest of honour this evening.'

Polite applause rippled around the room as the man stepped up to the podium. Natalie glanced at Rafferty and bit back a chuckle when she saw the expression of utter boredom on his face. It was the local business association's annual dinner, a lengthy affair which normally she avoided attending. She hadn't been planning on going that night either, until Rafferty had bulldozed his way into her office and she'd realised it would be the perfect way to pay him back. If he had all those preconceived ideas about how she'd been spending her time recently, why disabuse him?

He must have sensed she was watching him because he suddenly turned and her heart missed a beat when she saw the awareness in his eyes. She'd pulled out all the stops that night and knew she looked her best. The red gown she was wearing was one of her favourites, although she'd never worn it before when she'd been out with Rafferty. Most of the time they'd spent together had been at some disaster spot or other and there'd been few opportunities there to dress up. It struck her all of a sudden just how little time they'd spent doing the normal things a couple usually did together. Their relationship had revolved around their work and they'd just snatched the odd hour as and when they could.

Would things have turned out differently if they'd had more time to themselves? she wondered. Everyone was under a lot of pressure when they were away on a mission. Consequently emotions ran high, and it could explain why they'd never been able to reach a compromise.

'How much longer do we have to stay here?' he demanded, leaning over so that he could whisper the question in her ear.

'It's not the done thing to leave before the main guest has finished speaking,' she informed him tersely. She'd always believed that their failure to agree had been because of his stubbornness and it was worrying to wonder if she'd been wrong to hold him solely responsible when there might have been other factors involved.

'It will be midnight at this rate before he runs out of steam,' Rafferty declared in disgust. 'Who on earth is interested in the profit and loss ratios that can be achieved in various European countries?'

'A lot of people. You might believe that making a profit is the devil's work but your views aren't shared by the majority of people here tonight.'

'I never said it was wrong to make a profit,' he denied, frowning.

'No? It certainly sounded like it to me earlier today.'

She smiled sweetly at him then turned her attention to the speaker but it was difficult to concentrate when her mind kept returning to the thought that she might have been wrong to blame Rafferty for their problems. It was a relief when the speech ended and everyone started talking. Natalie knew most of the people on their table because she'd met them when she'd acted as hostess for her father. Richard Palmer was a renowned host and his cocktail parties were always well attended.

The man on her right asked her how her father was so she turned to speak to him, aware that Rafferty was talking to the woman seated next to him. She could just catch snippets of their conversation, something about an opera which had been a sell-out. Someone else joined in, adding their comments on the production, until the whole table ended up discussing its merits. Natalie smiled when a woman seated opposite her asked if she'd seen it.

'I've not had time, I'm afraid. I've been too busy trying to find my way around Palmer's so I've not been to the theatre for ages.'

The woman smiled sympathetically then turned her attention to Rafferty. 'And how about you, Dr Rafferty? Have you managed to get tickets for it yet? It's a marvellous production, so much better than Antonini's version. If you saw it, I'm sure you'd agree.'

'I'm afraid I'm not really an opera buff,' Rafferty replied evenly. 'My visits to the *theatre* tend to have a rather different purpose behind them.'

Everyone laughed at the quip, as he'd obviously intended them to. However, Natalie could tell there was something bothering him. She frowned to herself, because she had no idea what was wrong. They'd just been making conversation, the kind of small talk that usually happened at these events, so why did Rafferty look so on edge?

The band began to play so, under cover of the general hubbub that broke out as people got up to dance, she leant over and asked him, 'Are you all right?'

'Fine. Why shouldn't I be?'

His tone was bland enough but she could tell from the tautness of his jaw that he was still very tense. She shrugged, feeling her way with care because she didn't want to make matters worse by saying the wrong thing. 'You just looked a bit...well, *uneasy* when we were talking about the opera.'

'Did I?' He shrugged. 'Probably because there wasn't a lot I could contribute. Opera is something that has passed me by, I'm afraid.'

'Oh, I see.'

Natalie wasn't sure she did see, but there was little she could say when he obviously didn't want to talk about it any more. Maybe he wasn't interested in opera, as he'd claimed, but his reaction seemed to her to be just a little too much. She breathed a sigh of relief when a waiter appeared and informed her there was a phone call for her in Reception because it provided a welcome distraction.

She quickly excused herself, as she had a good idea who it might be. Since she'd been back in London, she'd been helping out at a drop-in clinic for the many homeless teenagers who lived on the streets of the city. The clinic was staffed by a team of volunteer nurses and doctors and provided a lifeline for the youngsters who were often loath to seek medical help elsewhere. Although she wasn't due to work that night, she'd made sure they had the phone number of the hotel where the dinner was being held in case anything cropped up. The reception staff had transferred the call to a private booth in the foyer so she went straight there and picked up the receiver.

'Natalie Palmer.'

'Hi, Natalie, it's Helen. I'm sorry to phone you but we have a bit of a problem. It's Danny Kennedy and he's in a pretty bad way, I'm afraid.'

Natalie sighed. Danny was a regular visitor to the clinic. He was in his early teens and had run away from home after his parents had split up and his mother's new partner had beaten him up. He'd suffered from asthma all his life and living on the streets was making the problem worse.

'Has he been taking his medication?' she asked worriedly.

'He says he has but it doesn't sound like it to me,' Helen explained. 'I really think he should be admitted to hospital but he's refusing to go. I thought you might be able to persuade him to see sense.'

'I'll try.' She checked her watch. 'If I leave straight away, I should be with you in about ten minutes' time. If he gets any worse, though, call an ambulance and we'll argue about it later.'

'Will do. Thanks, Natalie.'

Natalie left the booth, trying to decide what she should tell Rafferty. He had no idea that she'd been working at the clinic since she'd come back to London and she wasn't sure if she wanted him to know about it either.

'Is everything all right?'

She jumped when the subject of her thoughts suddenly materialised at her side. She turned to face him, feeling her heart give an appreciative little flutter before she could stop it. The formal dinner suit he was wearing made the most of his dark good looks, emphasising the width of his shoulders and the trimness of his waist. Rarely had she seen him wearing anything other than scrubs or jeans and she had to admit that he looked great. However, how he looked wasn't the issue. She was more concerned about what she was going to tell him.

Her father had instilled into her a sense of duty from an early age. He had insisted that it wasn't enough just to be rich and that she had to prove her worth by giving something back to the world. Natalie had never had a problem with that idea because it wasn't in her nature to idle away her time. She enjoyed helping people, and loved nursing, so she had tried to live up to his high expectations of her. However, whilst she was prepared to accept that kind of attitude from her father, she didn't see why she should have to justify herself to Rafferty. She was still smarting at the thought that he valued her more as a nurse than anything else, and certainly didn't intend to make it appear as though she was trying to curry favour with him!

'Something has cropped up and I'm going to have to leave,' she said shortly, heading for the cloakroom.

'It's not your father, is it? He hasn't taken a turn for the worse?'

'No, nothing like that,' she replied evasively, handing her ticket to the attendant.

'But it must be important if you're rushing off.'

'It is.'

Natalie took her coat from the woman and hurried across the foyer but if she'd hoped to deter him, obviously she'd failed. He followed her outside, his expression turning thunderous as he watched her flag down a passing taxi.

'Are you going to tell me what's going on?'

'No.' She opened the cab door and got in. 'I'll see you in the office tomorrow morning. Your pass should be ready so you'll just need to ask the staff on Reception for it when you arrive.'

She started to shut the door but he was too quick for her. His green eyes flashed as he bent and looked at her.

'I'm asking you one last time where you're going, Natalie.'

'And I'm telling you one last time that it hasn't anything to do with you. You gave up the right to have a say in what I do when you told me that our relationship wasn't going to work.'

She went to close the door again and this time he didn't try to stop her. She told the driver the address of the clinic then sat back in the seat. She could feel Rafferty staring at her as the cab drove away but she didn't look at him, didn't dare in case she weakened. She loved him so much, but it wasn't enough. He had to love her too—unconditionally and without any strings attached—and the likelihood of that happening seemed even more remote after what he'd told her that day.

She closed her eyes, feeling the pain welling inside her again. She might be a rich man's daughter, she might be a nurse, but she was first and foremost a woman and she wanted a man who would love her for herself.

Helen must have been watching for her to arrive because she came hurrying out of the clinic as soon as the taxi drew up. She whistled when Natalie turned round after paying the driver.

'Wowee! That's some dress, girl. You must have really socked it to him in that get-up. I bet he's still reeling!'

Natalie's mood immediately lifted and she laughed. She'd become good friends with the attractive Anglo-Caribbean nurse since she'd been working at the clinic and was hoping to persuade her to join Worlds Together at some point. 'If he is then he managed to hide it pretty well. The last I saw of him, he was glaring after the taxi and looking as though he was about to spit tacks!'

'No wonder.' Helen grinned as she opened the clinic's door and ushered her inside. 'The poor guy probably thought he was in for a night of passion when he saw you in that outfit, and what do you go and do? Only run out on him!' She shook her head. 'That wasn't very kind, was it?'

'Tough. He shouldn't have counted his chickens, should he?'

Natalie refused to feel guilty, because in her opinion she had nothing to feel guilty about. She hadn't promised Rafferty a night of passion—*despite* what he might have been expecting.

Her heart lurched at the thought of how the evening might have ended if the situation had been different. The one thing they'd never had any problem with had been sex, and she doubted if either of them could create the same kind of magic with anyone else. However, although the physical side of their relationship may have been perfect, the rest of it certainly hadn't, she reminded herself. There would need to be a lot of changes made before she would consider jumping into bed with Rafferty again…

'So how's Danny doing?' she said, swiftly changing the subject. The odds on her and Rafferty sleeping together again were approximately zero so there was no point even thinking about it. 'Any improvement yet?'

'No. If anything, I'd say he's slightly worse.' Helen sighed as she pushed open the door that separated the reception area from the treatment rooms.

The clinic was based in one of the arches beneath a railway bridge and the sound of the trains thundering overhead provided a constant background noise. The space had been used as a garage before it had been taken over by the clinic and on warm evenings the smell of diesel still seeped from the walls. Bright strip-lighting and plenty of white paint had helped to dispel the gloom, however, and the staff did their best to make everyone feel welcome. Maybe it wasn't the ideal place for a medical centre but the youngsters came, and that was what mattered most of all.

'I've put Danny in the end cubicle because it's a bit quieter down there,' Helen informed her. 'Piers was supposed to be here tonight but he phoned just before you arrived to say that he's having to work a double shift because they're short-staffed at the hospital.'

'So that means Danny hasn't seen a doctor yet?' Natalie clarified.

'Not yet.' Helen glanced round when one of the other nurses called over to her. 'I'll see what Suzy wants then come and find you.'

'Fine.'

Natalie made her way down the long, arched room to the very end cubicle, which was actually more substantial than it sounded, with solid hardboard walls and a proper door. She tapped on the door and went in, smiling as she saw Danny's eyes widen in surprise when he saw what she was wearing.

'I only wear this outfit for my very favourite patients, I'll have you know,' she told him, laughing as she twirled round so he could get a good look at her gown.

He removed the oxygen mask he was wearing and smiled shyly back at her. It had been a couple of weeks since he'd visited the clinic and she could tell that he'd lost a lot of weight in that time. He was wearing an old T-shirt and she could see how his chest was heaving from the effort of drawing air into his lungs.

'The other guys will be really jealous,' he wheezed.

'And so they should be,' she retorted, going over to the bed. She took hold of his wrist and checked his pulse, frowning when she felt how fast it was racing. It was obviously a very bad attack and she really couldn't understand why it had happened. 'So when did this all start?'

'A couple of hours ago...although I've not felt well for a few days,' he admitted reluctantly.

'And have you been taking your medication like I told you to do?' she asked, sitting down on the side of the bed.

'Uh-huh,' he muttered, avoiding her eyes.

Natalie sighed. 'Look, Danny, I'm not going to tell you off if you haven't been taking it...well, not much, at least. But I need to find out why this has happened tonight. I thought we'd sorted you out the last time you came to see us but maybe the drugs we prescribed for you aren't doing their job properly and we need to try you on something else.'

'The drugs are OK,' he mumbled, but she could see tears welling into his eyes.

She squeezed his hand, hating to see him looking so upset. He was far too young to be living on the streets and she wished she could do more to help him, but she'd been warned before she'd started working at the clinic that she mustn't try to interfere. A lot of the youngsters they treated would stop attending the clinic if they thought there was a chance that the authorities would be contacted.

'So what's the problem?' she asked gently. 'If the drugs have been working, why have you had such a bad attack tonight?'

'Because I haven't taken my tablets for the past couple of days,' Danny admitted. 'I...um...lost them.'

'Lost them?' She stared at him in surprise. 'But I thought you always kept them in your pocket so they'd be safe.'

'I do. I mean, I did…' He tailed off and she shook her head when she realised what had happened.

'Did someone take the drugs off you, Danny?'

'Yes,' he whispered, biting his lip.

Natalie tried to hide her frustration although it wasn't the first time something like this had happened. Life on the streets was tough and drugs of any description were a valuable commodity. Several of the youngsters they'd treated recently had experienced the same thing and it was starting to look as though their patients were being targeted deliberately.

'Did you go to the police and report what had happened?' she asked without much hope.

Danny shook his head. 'They'd have beaten me up again if I'd done that.'

'Again? Are you saying that the people who took your medication beat you up as well?'

'Yes. They kicked me about and that's why I gave them the tablets. I think they might have busted one of my ribs because it's been really hurting.'

'And I don't suppose you had anyone look at it, did you?' Natalie said wearily, and he shook his head. 'Right, I need to check you over but first of all I want you to put that oxygen mask back on.'

She helped the boy replace the mask then unbuttoned his shirt, grimacing when she saw the yellowing remains of bruising down the left side of his chest. He'd obviously taken a severe beating because she could tell how much it hurt when she gently explored the area. He'd definitely broken a rib—possibly two—and she wished she could get hold of the thugs who'd done this to him.

She buttoned his shirt again and looked sternly at him. 'You've got at least one broken rib and you should have come to the clinic if you didn't want to go to hospital.'

'It hurt too much to walk,' he mumbled through the mask.

'I bet it did.' She looked round when Helen appeared. 'Young Danny here has a broken rib. Apparently, someone beat him up and took his medication off him. That explains why he's in such a state tonight.'

'That's the third time this week it's happened to one of our kids!' Helen exclaimed angrily. 'What is the world coming to?'

'I shudder to think. Anyway, I think he should be checked over by a doctor—' She broke off when Danny suddenly interrupted her.

'I don't want to go to the hospital! They'll give me another thumping if they think I've told on them.'

There was genuine terror in his voice and Natalie frowned. 'Is that what they told you would happen?'

'Yes. And they meant it, too. They've given other people a real going over when they thought they'd told on them.'

Danny looked exhausted when he'd finished speaking and Natalie realised that it would do more harm than good to try and make him reconsider. She drew Helen aside while they decided what they should do.

'Is there any chance we could keep him here overnight? I know we don't usually allow anyone to stay in the clinic but Danny's far too ill to go back on the streets tonight. I'd feel much happier if he was in hospital, of course, but we can't force him to go if he doesn't want to.'

'I suppose we could bend the rules just this once,' Helen agreed reluctantly. 'Although obviously we can't leave him here on his own. He seems a nice enough kid but you just never know, so someone will have to stay here with him.'

'I'll stay,' Natalie offered immediately.

'Are you sure? It's not even your night to work...'

'That doesn't matter. It was my decision to keep him here so I should be the one to stay with him.' She shrugged. 'Anyway, I've nothing better to do so I may as well be here as at home.'

'Fair enough, although it's not what you'd call a fair trade, is it?' Helen grinned when she looked blankly at her. 'A night in the clinic instead of a night of passion?'

Natalie laughed dutifully. It wasn't worth explaining that a night of passion hadn't been in the offing. She found something more suitable to wear than the red evening gown and changed in one of the empty cubicles. The clinic was open until midnight every day of the week and there was a steady stream of youngsters needing attention until they shut up shop.

She said goodbye to the others then went to check on Danny. He still didn't look well and once again she tried to persuade him to let her phone for an ambulance, but he was adamant that he didn't want to go to hospital. In the end she had to bow to his wishes, although she made up her mind that if he hadn't improved by the morning, she would have to reconsider.

She went into the next cubicle and lay down on the bed, fully dressed, and dozed until it was time to check on him again. That set the pattern for the night and she was glad when morning came. The clinic opened again at eight and she had everything ready when the day staff arrived.

Danny seemed a little better thanks to the drugs and a night spent in a proper bed so Natalie handed him over to Sam Cummins, one of their volunteer doctors, then changed back into her evening dress and went home, to find Rafferty sitting on her doorstep. She took a deep breath as she got out of the cab because if the expression on his face was anything to go by, he wasn't in the best of moods either.

Rafferty had gone straight home after Natalie had driven away in the taxi and had spent the night pacing the floor of his flat. The thought that she was meeting some other guy had been more than he could bear but how else could he explain why she'd refused to tell him where she was going? By the time dawn broke, he had been almost beside himself with frustration and had known he had to do something to rectify the situation. Maybe it wasn't too late for them to work things out? Maybe they could find a solution to their problems if they tried hard enough? Maybe…

To hell with maybe, he'd thought grimly, heading for the door. He was going to see her and get this sorted out!

He took a taxi to her home and rang the bell, unsurprised when he didn't get an answer. He sat down on the step to wait—she would have to come home at some point. This area of London was one of the most exclusive parts of the city and he sighed as he looked at the expensive houses surrounding the elegant, tree-lined square. He'd worked hard to reach his present position as chief of surgery at one of London's most prestigious teaching hospitals, but even on his salary, he couldn't have afforded to buy a property here. Only the very rich could afford to live in these houses and it was an unwelcome reminder of the difference between his and Natalie's lifestyles. How could he hope to make their relationship work when they were worlds apart?

The thought nagged away at him so that by the time she appeared, a couple of hours later, he'd reached boiling point. He stood up as she crossed the pavement, feeling his heart ache when he saw the shadows under her beautiful grey eyes. She looked as though she hadn't slept a wink and it confirmed his suspicions about what she'd been doing. She'd spent the night with another man and the thought was like rubbing salt into an open wound.

'I thought I'd already explained that I would see you in the office,' she said coolly, taking her front-door key out of her bag.

'You did.' Rafferty ground his teeth because he wasn't accustomed to being spoken to in that offhand fashion. 'However, I'm sure you would prefer to keep your private life away from the office, wouldn't you?'

'That's very thoughtful of you, Rafferty.' She smiled at him as though she was acknowledging a favour from an underling and his already-volatile temper rocketed another few notches up the scale. 'However, quite apart from the fact that my private life has nothing to do with you, I really don't have time to talk to you about it right now. I need to get ready for work, so whatever you want to say to me will have to wait, I'm afraid.'

She opened the front door but if she thought he was going to meekly turn tail and leave, she could think again. Rafferty followed her into the house, ignoring her protests as he closed the door behind him.

'If you don't have much time to spare, I'll keep it brief. Where were you last night, Natalie?'

'I really don't think it has anything to do with you.'

'Were you with someone else?' he demanded as jealousy got the better of him. He'd spent the whole damned night imagining what she'd got up to after she'd left him at that dinner. He'd thought about it so much, in fact, that it was picture-perfect in his head: She'd gone to some other guy's home where they'd had a glass of wine and discussed subjects they were both knowledgeable about, like opera for instance. He hadn't a clue about opera or ballet or any other such elitist topics, but he'd bet his last pound that *this* fellow knew everything there was to know about them. Then after the wine had been drunk and the conversation had petered out, no doubt they'd found other ways to entertain themselves… In bed!

'Someone else,' she repeated woodenly.

'Yes!' He glared at her, wondering why she was trying to pretend that she didn't understand when it was perfectly clear to him what had been going on. 'You spent the night with some other guy, didn't you? And that's why you wouldn't tell me where you were going last night.'

'I see. You seem to have it all worked out, don't you? I wouldn't tell you where I was going—*ipso facto*, I must have been seeing someone else.'

Rafferty frowned when he heard the hurt in her voice because it was the last thing he'd expected to hear. 'Are you saying that you didn't spend the night with someone else?'

'Not at all.' She placed her bag on the gilded console table beside the front door and looked steadily at him. 'If there's nothing else that you wanted to say, I really think it would be best if you left now.'

'I'm not leaving until we've sorted this out,' he said firmly, as much for his own benefit as hers. So maybe it felt as though he'd been kicked in the guts to have his suspicions confirmed but he would get over it. Eventually. It was far more important that they sorted this out before any more mistakes were made, because that was what last night had been, of course: a mistake. If Natalie had spent the night with another man, it was because she'd thought *their* relationship was over. But was that what he *really* wanted?

They'd split up before, of course—several times—but had always got back together. Rafferty realised with a sinking heart that he'd assumed it would happen this time, too. However, it appeared that he might have taken too much for granted. Natalie obviously believed it was the end for them because she was looking for someone to replace him, and the thought was too much to bear. He didn't want to lose her! He had to find a way to convince her that their relationship could still work…

Rafferty jumped when there was a sudden thunderous pounding on the door behind him. It sounded as though they were being attacked by a hoarde of marauding invaders but Natalie—surprisingly—didn't appear the least concerned as she stepped around him and calmly opened the front door.

His jaw dropped when he saw a couple of burly security guards standing on the step, because it was like watching a rerun of what had happened in her office the day before.

'We have reason to believe that an alarm has been triggered in this house,' one of the men curtly informed them, stepping into the hall.

'I didn't hear an alarm,' Rafferty said, glancing at Natalie in surprise.

'It's a silent alarm—an extra security measure my father had put in place in case anyone forces his way in when I'm entering the house.' She smiled sweetly as she nodded to the men. 'I did tell you that it would be better if you left.'

Before he knew what was happening, Rafferty suddenly found himself being hustled out of the door. There was a van parked by the kerb and he swore when he realised the guards were taking him to it. He shot a glance over his shoulder in time to see Natalie waggle her fingers at him, then the men were pushing him into the back of the van.

He sat down on the seat as he was instructed to do because it wouldn't achieve anything to argue with them. However, he found it difficult to believe that she'd pulled the same stunt on him again. By the time the van drew up in front of the headquarters of the security firm, he was beside himself with fury and it didn't help when he was brusquely informed that Miss Palmer had telephoned to say that, as she didn't intend to press charges, he was free to leave.

Rafferty went back to his flat and made straight for his bedroom, where he took a suitcase out of the cupboard. He'd arranged to take some leave after he'd returned from Guatemala so he wasn't due back at the hospital until the end of the month. Although he hadn't planned on going away, a break would do him good. A few days' R & R might help to restore some order to his life…

And what about Natalie? a small voice taunted. Was he going to give up at the first hurdle, or was he going to do what he'd set out to do and get her back to nursing? When push came to shove, was he a man or a mouse?

His mouth compressed because he'd never considered himself to be a coward before. However, cowardice came in many different guises and he couldn't deny that he was terrified of getting hurt. He had always guarded his emotions but he must put aside his fears if he was to achieve his objective. Natalie was a superb nurse and he had to convince her that she was wasting her talents. Just because he couldn't handle the thought of her being with another man, that wasn't a good enough reason to give up and he would bitterly regret it in years to come. He owed it to the rest of the Worlds Together team to bring her back into the fold.

He shoved the suitcase back into the cupboard and slammed the door. If Natalie thought she'd got rid of him then she was in for a shock!

CHAPTER THREE

'THERE'S a board meeting at two so I'll take an early lunch today. Can you make sure that everyone has a copy of that report I prepared, please, Janet?'

Natalie sighed as her secretary assured her it would be done and hurried away. It had been difficult to concentrate on work since she'd arrived at the office. She kept thinking about what had happened that morning and the awful things Rafferty had said to her. How could he believe that she'd slept with someone else? Didn't he know that she loved him and that the thought of sleeping with someone else was totally abhorrent? Or was he judging her by his own actions perhaps?

She got up and went to the window, too on edge to sit while thoughts like that plagued her. It was a beautiful day yet she could derive none of her usual pleasure from the view over the river. Had Rafferty slept with someone else since they'd parted, and was that why he'd leapt to such a conclusion that morning?

She didn't want to believe it but neither could she dismiss the idea out of hand. After all, Rafferty was a very attractive man and there would be no shortage of volunteers if he needed company. Had he found solace after their break-up in some other woman's arms?

'Sorry I'm late. I got held up but I'll make sure I'm here on time in future.'

Natalie swung round when Rafferty suddenly appeared in her office. She'd never expected him to turn up after the latest stunt she'd pulled and it was hard to hide her consternation as he came towards her.

'You were expecting me, I hope?' he said smoothly, one dark brow arching. 'There haven't been any changes made to our arrangements?'

'I…um…no. Of course not,' she replied testily, immediately on the defensive.

'Good.' He stopped in front of her, smiling as he fingered the badge pinned to the lapel of his suit jacket. 'I see I've been awarded top-level security clearance. I'm flattered by your faith in my integrity.'

'You'll need full clearance if you're going to complete this challenge I've set you,' she informed him curtly. She went back to her desk and sat down, riffling through the letters Janet had left for her to sign while she tried to get herself under control. If Rafferty could handle this situation, so could she.

'So what's on the agenda today?'

He pulled up a chair and sat down opposite her, his face betraying nothing more than friendly interest, and Natalie frowned. It was completely out of character for him to take this relaxed approach after what she'd done, so it was hard to know how to respond.

'There's a board meeting this afternoon,' she explained, deciding it was easier to follow his lead and behave as though nothing had happened.

'Something to look forward to,' he observed dryly, crossing one long leg over the other and treating her to a condescending smile.

'It should be interesting,' she said evenly, refusing to rise to the bait.

'Hmm, I suppose it depends what you consider interesting.'

Natalie bit back her sharp retort although she knew the meeting was going to be a difficult one. It had been called by a member of the board who was strongly opposed to the support Palmer's gave to Worlds Together as well as their other charitable ventures. It would need careful handling to convince everyone to continue funding the projects but she didn't intend to explain that to him.

'It does indeed. However, the board meeting isn't until two o'clock so this morning I was planning on visiting the research lab. We may as well go straight up there now, in fact.'

'I didn't realise there was a laboratory in the building,' he said in surprise as she stood up.

'We do most of our major research here, although we do have other laboratories, of course. They're used mainly for testing the various products we manufacture.'

She led the way from the office and went straight to the lift. 'Security is always a major issue when you're developing a new drug and we've found it best to keep everything under one roof. There's less risk of any information leaking out this way.'

'It makes sense. Are you working on something new at the moment?' he asked, and she smiled faintly when she heard the curiosity in his voice. Despite his determination to view Palmer's in the worst possible light, he couldn't help being interested.

'We're developing a new drug to treat Hansen's disease.' The lift arrived and she stepped inside, pressing the button for the sixth floor, which was where the research laboratory was sited.

'Because of the increased resistance to dapsone?' he queried, and she nodded.

'Yes. A lot of people don't realise that leprosy is still a major health issue in many parts of the world, like Africa and Asia. They assume it was eradicated centuries ago but, sadly, that isn't the case. As you know, the bacteria that cause the disease have become increasingly resistant to dapsone and it's been standard practice for a number of years to prescribe a combination of dapsone, rifampicin and clofazimine to treat the disease. Obviously, this increases the treatment cost per patient quite considerably and in turn puts an added burden on the health-care budgets of the countries involved. We're hoping this new drug we're developing will do the job on its own and cut costs.'

'It would be a step in the right direction if it works, but surely it's an extremely costly undertaking to develop a new drug? Clinical trials alone must cost a fortune and I can't see Palmer's or any other pharmaceutical company wanting to spend millions developing a product which might take years to pay for itself. Leprosy is a disease of the developing world so sales of the drug will be restricted to some of the poorest countries.'

'It's part of our charitable programme,' she explained, exiting the lift when they reached their floor. She led him along the corridor and stopped outside the door to the lab, placing her palm on the screen set into the wall beside it. All the doors on this floor were opened by means of a sophisticated bio-scanning system and once the computer had confirmed that her palmprint matched the one stored in its database, they were admitted.

'And do you develop many drugs through your charitable programme?' Rafferty asked quietly, following her into the changing area. Conditions inside the lab were sterile and everyone entering had to wear a protective suit to prevent contamination. Natalie took one off a shelf and handed it to him before she answered the question.

'As many as we can. Obviously, the firm has to make a profit before it can invest time and money in a new project such as this. Basically, it's a question of finding the right balance.'

'I hadn't realised Palmer's was so committed to its charitable work,' he confessed, taking off his jacket and hanging it on a peg.

'When my grandfather founded the company, he decided that a percentage of its profits should be used to help the least fortunate people in the world. My father has tried to uphold that principle since he took over.'

'But it's not always been an easy thing to do?' he suggested astutely, stepping into the suit and zipping it up.

'No. There are factions within the company that would like to see the system changed as soon as possible.'

She took off her shoes and slipped into a suit. There were paper bootees to wear with it so she found a large pair for Rafferty and gave them to him then found a smaller pair for herself.

'And is that why you decided to stand in for your father while he recovered from his heart attack?'

'Yes. I didn't want Dad worrying that changes might be instigated in his absence. All it would take is a majority vote of no confidence from the board members and he could find himself overruled.'

'You really think they would do that?' he exclaimed.

'Yes.' She laughed shortly. 'We're talking about an awful lot of money, don't forget. If you add up what Palmer's invests in its charitable programme each year, it runs into millions. There are a lot of people who would like to see that money spent on something else.'

'I had no idea the situation was so difficult. I can understand now why you were so anxious to return to London.'

'I knew my father wouldn't be able to rest if he was worrying about what was going on within the company and that certainly wouldn't have helped his recovery.'

'I wish you'd told me all this before.'

'I didn't see the point.' She shrugged when he looked at her in surprise. 'It wasn't as though we were on the best of terms when it happened.'

She turned to enter the laboratory but Rafferty stopped her and she saw the regret in his eyes.

'I never meant to hurt you, Natalie. I just wanted to do what was right.'

'And telling me that we didn't have a future was the right thing to do?'

'I thought it was, but it wasn't easy, if that's what you imagine. I just knew that we couldn't keep on tearing each other apart the way we'd been doing. We kept going round and round in circles and never getting anywhere.'

'We didn't have to *get* anywhere. That's the whole point!' She gripped his arms, desperate to make him understand. 'The fact that my family has all this money doesn't matter, Rafferty. It doesn't change who we are or how we feel about each other.'

'I wish I could believe that…'

'You could if you wanted to but maybe it's easier to blame the difference in our backgrounds than admit the truth.'

'What truth?'

'That you never really loved me enough to put aside your principles.'

She let him go and went to the door, repeating the procedure of scanning her palmprint. Rafferty didn't say a word and his silence seemed to confirm that she'd been right about why they'd never been able to resolve their differences. It had had nothing to do with the lack of time they'd spent together or the constant pressure of their work, and she couldn't believe why she hadn't realised it before when it was so simple. If Rafferty had *really* loved her, he would have done everything in his power to keep her.

Rafferty knew he'd made a mistake by not denying the accusation but it had caught him flat-footed. How could Natalie think that he cared more about his principles than he did about her? He was determined to set her straight as he followed her into the lab but he was thwarted when one of the technicians spotted them and came hurrying over.

'Dr Khan is in his office, Miss Palmer.'

'Thank you, Rudi.'

Natalie turned to him and Rafferty felt his heart ache when he saw the pain in her eyes. It was obvious how hurt she was and the need to explain that she'd got things wrong was overwhelming.

'Look, Natalie—' he began, but she didn't allow him to finish.

'I'm sure you would like to meet the head of our research programme, wouldn't you?'

She didn't wait for him to answer as she led the way across the huge, open-plan room. Rafferty cursed under his breath but short of making a scene there was little he could do but follow her. She stopped outside a door at the far side of the laboratory and knocked before going into the office. There was a small, rather plump man sitting behind the desk, and he smiled in delight when he saw her.

'Natalie! How lovely to see you, my dear!' he exclaimed, leaping to his feet. 'I was hoping you would find the time to call in today because I have some exciting news.'

'Don't tell me that you've made a breakthrough at last with the new drug?'

'Let's just say that it's looking very promising.'

'That's wonderful news, Sanjay.' She turned and Rafferty experienced a little spurt of irritation when he saw her smile fade as she looked at him. 'Dr Khan has been working on that new drug I told you about.'

'For Hansen's disease.' He smiled pleasantly as he offered the other man his hand. He had no intention of letting her see that her coolness had upset him. 'Michael Rafferty. I'm delighted to meet you, Dr Khan.'

'The pleasure is all mine, Dr Rafferty, I assure you,' the man replied warmly as they shook hands. 'I've heard a lot about your work for Worlds Together. You and your team do an excellent job, if I may say so.'

'Thank you. However, we wouldn't be able to do our job half as successfully if we didn't have the right drugs available to us. The work you do in your own field is every bit as important.'

'Thank you.' Dr Kahn graciously accepted the compliment then turned to Natalie again. 'Would you and Dr Rafferty care to see the results of our most recent trials?'

'That would be wonderful, Sanjay. Thank you.'

Once again the man was treated to a megawatt smile but this time Rafferty was prepared for it. He followed them from the office, wondering if she was doing it deliberately to make him feel bad. He couldn't blame her if she was, because she had every right to be annoyed with him. He made up his mind that he would set her straight as soon as he got her on her own but it proved to be far more difficult than he'd anticipated.

They stayed over an hour in the lab and when they got back to her office, there was someone from the accounts department waiting to see her. Rafferty listened with mounting impatience while they discussed the quarterly figures. It was double Dutch to him, although Natalie seemed to understand what was being said, and her grasp of the complexities of the business surprised him. He found himself pondering on it as the meeting with the accountant was followed by one with the head of marketing. Once again she asked pertinent questions and he could tell from the responses she received that her opinion was valued highly.

It forced him to re-evaluate his opinion of what she'd been doing recently. She hadn't been wasting her time, as he'd assumed. She'd been making a positive contribution to the running of the company. It made him see just how difficult it was going to be to persuade her to give up the job so that by the time they broke for lunch, he was in a quandary. However, uppermost on his mind was the need to sort out the misunderstanding that had arisen that morning. It was *because* he loved her that he'd stuck to his principles, not the other way round, as she believed, so as soon as they were alone, he got straight to the point.

'I need to talk to you about what happened earlier today. Perhaps we could go out for lunch while we discuss it?'

'I'm sorry but I've already made plans,' she said coolly, taking her jacket off the back of her chair. She was wearing a black trouser suit that day and he couldn't help thinking how elegant she looked. He was more used to seeing her in jeans and T-shirt, or scrubs after a stint in Theatre, so the contrast couldn't have been more marked. And all of a sudden he found himself beset by doubts once again.

Was it right to try and win her back when he could never give her the kind of life she was used to? He earned a good salary so they certainly wouldn't starve, but it wasn't just the money, of course. There were other considerations which he'd barely touched on because it was too painful to think about his past. He'd worked hard to hide his insecurities, had papered over the cracks with a layer of sophistication which fooled most people, but he knew his own shortcomings better than anyone else did. He might appear to the world as someone who was in charge of his life but it had been a hard battle to reach this point and it had left many scars.

He'd told Natalie very little about his childhood. He'd skirted around it by explaining that his parents were dead and she—not wanting to upset him—hadn't probed. She had no idea that he'd been brought up in care or that he had no recollection of the mother who had given him away as a toddler. She could have no conception of the kind of life he'd led, being shunted from one foster-home to another, because she'd always had family, friends, *roots*—all the things he lacked.

Everything he had today he'd earned. Everything he was he'd taught himself to be. He was proud of what he'd achieved but his life was so far removed from hers that they had no common ground, nothing to provide a solid basis for their relationship. *Yes*, he loved her and, *yes*, he wanted her, but was it enough to make up for the rest? The fact that he couldn't answer that question with any degree of certainty was what made him hold back.

'It doesn't matter, then. What time's the meeting this afternoon?'

His tone was cool and gave no hint that it felt as though his guts were being ripped apart. If even *he* wasn't sure that he was the right man for her then what point would there be in trying to win her back? It might be better if he accepted that the distance between them was just too great and let her get on with her life. Without him.

'Two o'clock in the boardroom.' She took a folder off her desk and handed it to him and he steeled himself when he saw the concern in her eyes. 'Are you feeling all right, Rafferty? You look a little…stressed.'

'I'm fine.' He summoned a smile because if he confessed his fears, she would only tell him they didn't matter, and he couldn't afford to be swayed by her compassion. He needed to think about what he was doing and the consequences it could have. 'I'm probably suffering from an overdose of facts and figures. I don't know how you stand the boredom, Natalie, really I don't.'

Her face closed up as she picked up her bag. 'Each to his own, as they say. I'll see you later.'

She stalked past him with her head held high and Rafferty sighed. He certainly hadn't endeared himself to her with that crass remark and it hurt to know that she must think he was an insensitive clod, but what else could he have done? He needed to be sure that what he was doing was right. For her, not him.

He took the file over to the window and sat down. Even though he'd been forced to amend his opinion of the work she'd been doing recently, it didn't alter the fact that he still believed she should return to nursing. Nursing had always been more than just a job to her and he understood how passionately she felt about it because he felt the same way about what he did. Even if he achieved nothing else, he would make her see how important it was that she return to the career she loved.

Opening the file, he settled back in the chair. He was going to complete this challenge she'd set him and come through it with flying colours.

What *was* wrong with Rafferty?

On her way to the clinic that night, Natalie found herself thinking back over what had happened that afternoon. She'd been dreading the board meeting after those comments Rafferty had made and, in the event, it had been every bit as bad as she'd feared. Things had started out well enough: Rafferty had been at his most urbane when she'd introduced him to the rest of the board members. However, once the meeting had got under way, the situation had quickly deteriorated.

She sighed as she recalled Rafferty's response when one of the members who was most strongly opposed to Palmer's continuing support of its charitable ventures had voiced his opinion during the meeting. Before she'd had time to formulate a carefully worded reply, Rafferty had stepped in. He had been little short of rude as he'd told the man how many lives Worlds Together had saved and had then asked him if he thought he was getting value for money. What was the going rate for a human life? he'd demanded witheringly. One pound? Ten? A hundred?

Natalie had done her best to rescue the situation because making the other man look like a fool in front of his colleagues certainly wouldn't help her achieve what she wanted. She'd made an enemy that day because the fight had become personal now, and she couldn't understand why Rafferty had taken it to such extremes. Surely he could have got across his point with a little more diplomacy? Instead of which he'd gone straight for the jugular, attacking his opponent with a ruthlessness that had surprised her. It made her see that there was a lot she didn't know about him and it was worrying to admit it. She loved him with the whole of her heart, but how well did she really know him?

The taxi drew up outside the clinic and she was forced to cut short her musings as she paid the driver and got out. It was just gone seven and there were only a couple of patients in the waiting area when she went in. Piers Dutton, one of their junior doctors, was working that night and he grinned when she went through to the treatment room.

'Ah, I'm glad to see you've decided to relax the dress code, Nat. I was really worried when Sam told me that evening dress was now *de rigueur* for the staff. I'm still paying back my student loans and it would be a bit of a bind if I had to fork out for a dinner suit. Still, I didn't want to let the side down so I made a special effort just for you.'

He whipped off his sweatshirt to reveal an old-fashioned false shirtfront complete with bow-tie and studs. 'My grandfather let me borrow this especially for the occasion. What do you think?'

'Oh, ha-ha, very funny!' she retorted. Piers was in his second year as a house officer at St Bart's and an inveterate joker. They'd all been subjected to his pranks at one time or another and obviously it was her turn that night.

'We aim to please,' he responded, laughing.

Helen suddenly appeared from one of the cubicles and rolled her eyes when she saw what was going on. 'No wonder folk find it hard to believe he's a *proper* doctor. He acts more like a ten-year-old most of the time!'

'Now, now, you know you love me really,' Piers admonished her, planting a noisy kiss on Helen's cheek.

'I love my cat but he can be a real pest at times, too,' Helen retorted, pushing him away.

'A pest?' Piers let her go and clutched his chest. 'I'm gutted!'

'Not yet you aren't, so don't tempt me...'

Helen picked up a speculum and threatened him with it, and Natalie laughed. It was good to enjoy some light-hearted banter after what had gone on that day. After Piers had left, still muttering about the cruelty of womankind, she asked Helen if Danny Kennedy was still in the clinic.

'No, he left at lunchtime. Sam Cummins left a note in the office to say that Danny had claimed that he was feeling much better and wanted to leave. Sam said to tell you that he was sorry but there was no way he could stop him. The note's still there if you want me to find it for you.'

'No, it's fine. I just wanted to know how he was,' Natalie assured her, because there was no point wishing the boy had remained in the clinic for another night. They simply weren't equipped to act as a hospital, so all she could do was hope that the rest and the medication had done the trick.

There was no time to worry about it because they started to get busy and she soon had her hands full. She saw two young girls who had scabies—a skin infestation caused by mites burrowing under the skin to lay their eggs. The girls had been staying in a hostel and had probably caught the mites there.

Natalie made them both take a bath and scrub themselves with soft soap to open up the burrows, then applied a solution of benzyl benzoate all over their skin. She explained that they would need a second and a third treatment at twelve-hourly intervals to clear up the infestation and that they would have to make sure all their clothes as well as their bedding were washed thoroughly, otherwise it would happen again. Both girls were horrified at the thought of suffering a second infestation and when they left the clinic they were debating if they should go home to their parents. Obviously, the joys of living in London had begun to pale.

Natalie worked non-stop after that until they closed for the night. She shared a taxi part of the way home with Piers, dropping him off at the hospital where he had a room in the staff quarters. It was well past midnight by the time she unlocked the front door and she was worn out after the long day.

She made herself a mug of warm milk then ran a bath and relaxed in the steaming water, only getting out when her eyes started to close. She was in bed five minutes later and fell asleep almost as soon as her head touched the pillow, only to spend the night dreaming about Rafferty. Awake or asleep, her thoughts were never far away from him, it seemed.

CHAPTER FOUR

BY THE end of the week, Rafferty was growing increasingly frustrated. Although Natalie included him in everything to do with the running of the company, the rest of the time she completely cut him out. A couple of times he'd suggested they have lunch together but on each occasion she had claimed to have a prior engagement. She was deliberately keeping him at a distance and even though he still wasn't sure if it would be right to try and win her back, he would *at least* have liked the opportunity to do so.

Friday arrived and there was another round of meetings to get through—finance, marketing, a meeting with someone from the Committee on Safety of Medicines. By late afternoon he was starting to wonder if he could take much more and the thought of having to come back the following week and go through the same routine all over again was almost more than he could stand—yet what choice did he have? Unless he completed this challenge Natalie had set him, she would never agree to come on the next Worlds Together mission. Talk about being stuck between a rock and a hard place!

'That's just about it.' Natalie came back into the office after escorting the CSM man to the lift. 'It's been a busy week but we've achieved quite a lot, I'd say.'

'You've certainly got through enough meetings,' he observed dryly, standing up.

One delicate brow arched. 'You're not about to throw in the towel, are you?'

'No way. You're not getting rid of me that easily.' He

smiled mockingly. 'So if that was your plan, my sweet, it hasn't worked. I intend to see this through to the bitter end.'

'Obviously you're made of sterner stuff than I thought you were.'

She didn't deny his accusation and he sighed, because it was galling to know that he'd been right. She *had* been throwing obstacles in his path to get rid of him and it didn't make him feel great to know that. Just for a moment he found himself wondering if he was wasting his time, but his resolve firmed again. He would get her back to nursing if it was the last thing he did!

'So what's in your diary this weekend?' he asked, following her to the door. 'A garden party? A spot of polo? Or maybe a weekend shooting in the country? There must be lots of small furry animals that need terrorising.'

'I've not made up my mind yet,' she told him airily, waving goodbye to Janet who was still at her desk. 'It could be any of those or I might just stay home and wash my hair. How about you?'

'I've nothing planned,' he said tersely, because it was clear that she didn't intend to tell him how she was planning to spend her weekend. In the absence of any solid information, he could only make assumptions, and he was making them, too. Far too many assumptions, in fact. Was Natalie planning on spending the weekend with that guy she'd rushed off to see the other night?

Rafferty ground his teeth. The thought was enough to make him want to do something drastic but, logically, what could he do? Ban her from seeing the other fellow? He could imagine the reaction he'd get if he tried to do that.

'Rafferty!'

He looked up when he heard the exasperation in her voice and suddenly realised that they'd reached the ground floor while he'd been daydreaming and that she was waiting for him to get out of the lift. He strode past her, refusing to apologise for keeping her waiting when it was her own damned fault.

How could she sleep with another man after what they'd shared? How could she want someone else when what they'd had together had been so special? He would *never* want anyone the way he wanted her, and it was another thought that did little to enhance his already downbeat mood. Not only did Natalie no longer want him but he was doomed to spend the rest of his life in celibacy!

'Is something wrong?'

She paused on the step after they'd exited the building and stared at him. Rafferty did his best to arrange his features into a neutral expression. The last thing he wanted was her guessing how despondent he felt. Faint heart never won fair lady, or so the saying went, so he'd better get a grip.

'Not at all. I'm perfectly fine. In fact, I'd go so far as to say that I couldn't feel better.'

'Well, you certainly don't look it to me,' she snapped, marching down the steps ahead of him.

They crossed the car park at a rate of knots, only pausing when they came to a sleek little silver sports car parked in the chief executive's bay. It was a prestigious marque and the latest model to boot. Rafferty had seen the ads so he was well aware just how much the car must have cost, and it was like a naked flame being set to the touchpaper of his anger. How in heaven's name could he *hope* to compete on this level?

'We can't all be bright-eyed and bushy-tailed every minute of the day. Not everyone has your advantages, Natalie,' he said, shooting a speaking look at the expensive vehicle.

'So we're back to that, are we?' She unlocked the car and tossed her bag onto the passenger seat then glared at him. 'All you ever think about is money, Rafferty. Well, it doesn't buy happiness and if you haven't realised that by now, it's high time you did!'

She slid into the seat but Rafferty caught hold of the door before she could close it. 'I know money doesn't buy happiness, but it can and it does cause a lot of problems. Maybe it's time you thought about that, too.'

'I have thought about it. Believe me, I know the problems it can cause only too well!'

She laughed and he flinched when he heard the echo of pain in her voice. 'If you think it's easy growing up as the only child of a millionaire father, then you're mistaken. From the time I was old enough to understand, I never knew if people wanted to be friends with me because of who I was or how rich my parents were. And once I started dating it became a real minefield. It doesn't do much for your ego to wonder if a man finds you or your father's money more attractive!'

'You've always known that *I'm* not interested in your money,' he denied, stung by the insinuation.

'Maybe not interested in getting your hands on it—no. But it's always been a sticking point between us, hasn't it? Not that it matters now, because obviously you're less concerned about my family's money than you are about me proving my worth as a person.'

She went to close the door but he couldn't let her get away with that. Bending, he stared into her face, seeing the anguish in her eyes yet unsure what had caused it. 'What do you mean by that?'

'Nothing. It doesn't matter…'

'It does.'

He placed his hand over hers and felt his breath catch when she flinched. It took every scrap of control he could muster to carry on when what he wanted most was to haul her into his arms and kiss her until all these doubts had disappeared. However, in his heart he knew that sex wasn't the way to resolve this problem. If it had been, they would have sorted it out ages ago.

'What did you mean about proving your worth? I'm sorry, Natalie, but I don't understand.'

'I don't know why. You were the one who told me that I wasn't the woman you thought I was because I'd given up nursing.' She eased her hand out from beneath his and started the engine. 'Clearly, you measure my worth by the number of lives I save, so I'm sorry if I've disappointed you, Rafferty, but I'm no longer a nurse.'

Rafferty didn't know what to say to that. He'd never imagined for a second that his comment would have had this kind of effect on her. It had been a passing remark, stemming from frustration, and it had never been intended to hurt her. He placed his hand on her cheek and turned her face towards him so that she was forced to look at him.

'That wasn't what I meant, Natalie. I don't value you solely for the number of lives you save and I never have.'

'No?' She bit her lip and he groaned when he saw the tears that were welling into her eyes.

'No!' he repeated with renewed urgency, because it tore him apart to see her looking so upset.

'But you still believe I'm making a mistake by giving up nursing to work here.' She swept a hand around the car park. 'Big business isn't what you're about, is it, Rafferty? You can't see that sometimes you can help people—albeit indirectly.'

'It's hard,' he admitted, because it would be wrong to lie to her about something so important. 'However, I'm starting to change my views after what I've seen this week. Palmer's does a lot of good…'

'But you would never want to work for the firm, would you? You'd feel that you were selling out, which is what you accused me of doing.' She smiled sadly and it was almost too much to see the sorrow on her face. 'If that's your view then I'm sorry to have to tell you this, but it means you do value me more for my nursing skills than anything else.'

'How can you say that?' he exploded.

'Because it's true.' She touched him gently on the cheek, let her hand linger for a moment that was far too brief then placed it back on the steering-wheel. And there was something terrifyingly final about the gesture.

'If you loved me, Rafferty, it wouldn't matter what I did. You would value me for the person I am, and my family's money or my job wouldn't make a scrap of difference to you.'

'That's a very unrealistic attitude!' he protested, stung by the accusation. 'There are dozens of factors that need to be taken into account in a relationship.'

'That's your opinion, and you're entitled to it, of course. Mine is much simpler, I'm afraid.'

She gave him a sad little smile as she put the car into gear. Rafferty tried to think of something else to say but his thoughts seemed to be tumbling around inside his head like coloured chips inside a kaleidoscope. He watched in numb silence as she drove out of the car park and the fact that she didn't look back was another damning indictment of the damage he'd caused. Natalie couldn't even bear to look at him because she thought he didn't love her for the person she was, but he did. He did!

He took a deep breath and forced himself to calm down but nothing could ease the pain in his heart. He knew that he'd hurt her, knew, too, that it would take a lot to make her forgive him, but he would find a way to convince her not to give up on them...

And then what?

The question caught him unawares and he frowned because it seemed so trivial. Of course he knew the answer: it was simple. Once she'd forgiven him, then he would tell her that he loved her and...and...

What?

His brow furrowed because this second question—small

though it was—seemed far more difficult to answer. Everything was clear up to the point where he declared his love for Natalie, but the future was hazy after that.

He tried again. He would pluck up his courage and declare his love for her—that would be the first step. After that, he would explain his fears about her family being as rich as Croesus. Once he'd admitted that he was afraid he couldn't live up to her expectations, it would be easier. They would laugh about it together and she would assure him that he had no need to worry because it didn't matter…

Only it did.

It mattered to him, and not just the money either, but all the rest: his lack of roots; the absence of any family of his own; the way he'd been brought up. He cared about the whole damned lot and there was no point claiming that he didn't, was there? He wanted them to have a proper relationship, on an equal footing, and he wasn't sure if that was possible in the circumstances. He couldn't bear to think that one day—in that hazy future he was struggling to imagine—she might regret getting involved with him, couldn't stand to think that she might start to feel *ashamed* of him.

He groaned in despair. He was getting nowhere! Every time he tried to find a solution, another problem emerged. It wasn't just his feelings of inadequacy that stood in the way now, but also a fear of what the future might hold in store. He couldn't keep going round in circles like this, certainly couldn't bear to think that Natalie was trapped in a relationship which was going nowhere. He either had to resolve these issues once and for all or call it a day.

Natalie drove straight to the clinic after she left Palmer's. Even though she wasn't supposed to be on duty that night, she felt a desperate need to fill in the time and stop herself thinking about what had happened. Rafferty was deluding himself if he thought he loved her. Oh, maybe he *cared* about her and enjoyed having sex with her, but love?

No way was it love! Not true love, the sort of love her parents had had together, the kind of love one read about in books. *That* sort of love knew no boundaries, had no fears, overcame any obstacles. It withstood anything and everything that got in its way and it certainly didn't falter because of money or profession. True love was the most precious gift one person could give to another. And Rafferty didn't have a clue what it was about!

'My, someone's keen. Is this just a social visit or are you here to work?' Trish Burnham, one of their volunteer doctors, paused on her way to the treatment room when Natalie opened the front door.

'Work.' Natalie summoned a smile but her lips felt as though they were being tortured to death. If Rafferty didn't understand the true meaning of love, they didn't have a hope of sorting out this mess. 'Helen mentioned we were short-staffed tonight so I thought I'd offer my services.'

'Well, I certainly won't turn down such a wonderful offer,' Trish replied cheerfully.

Trish was in her fifties and had retired from medicine the previous year after working as a GP for over thirty years. When she'd found that the days had started to drag, she'd signed on at the clinic and now worked there every afternoon. She was the most experienced of all their doctors and an absolute mine of information. Now she laughed as Natalie followed her into the clinic.

'Although I have to say that most women your age would think twice about giving up their Friday evenings to work in this place.'

'I don't mind. I hadn't anything planned so I may as well make myself useful.'

Natalie didn't bother to explain that Friday was just another night to her. Most Fridays she sat in front of the television, too worn out after a week spent wrestling with Palmer's problems to think about going out.

How had Rafferty been spending his Friday evenings since they'd parted? she wondered all of a sudden, then blocked out the thought because she really didn't want to know.

She found a scrub suit and changed out of her office clothes then set to work. Trish asked her to clean and dress a cut that had gone septic so Natalie took the youngster into a cubicle.

'Just sit on the couch while I find what I need,' she told the boy, going over to the cupboard. She laid the trolley with antiseptic, cotton wool, plastic forceps and a selection of dressings then put on some gloves and went back to him.

'So how did you manage to do this to yourself, Ryan?' she asked, breaking open the cotton wool and fitting a piece into the disposable forceps. The wound was fairly deep and she felt the boy wince when she began to clean it, working outwards from the centre of the injury to avoid getting any more dirt into it. Although Ryan looked tidy enough, he smelt dreadful and his skin was ingrained with dirt so she made a note to give him the address of a local hostel where he could clean himself up.

'I cut it on some broken glass,' Ryan muttered, turning pale as he watched blood ooze from the wound.

'Don't watch if you hate the sight of blood,' she advised him, dropping the piece of cotton wool into the waste bag hanging on the end of the trolley. Picking up a clean piece, she worked her way around the other side of the wound, washing away the blood and dirt that had accumulated. 'Was it a broken bottle?'

'No, a window.'

Ryan shrugged when she looked at him in surprise. He'd claimed to be eighteen when he'd given his details to Annie, who was acting as both receptionist and triage nurse that night, but Natalie doubted if he was anywhere near as old as that. He looked more like fourteen to her and she bit back a sigh at the thought of a child that age living on the streets.

'Me and my mates have been squatting in a flat down by the station but the landlord has had the place boarded up so we had to find somewhere else to stay. We found a shop that's been closed up for years so we moved all our stuff in there.' The boy grimaced as he looked at his arm again. 'I cut myself when I was climbing through the window.'

'Well, fortunately it isn't very deep, although it's still a nasty injury,' Natalie said quietly. It wasn't her place to admonish him for breaking into the derelict shop. In any case, if there'd been enough decent accommodation for the youngsters they treated, they wouldn't be forced to resort to such methods.

'The doc said I might need stitches,' Ryan told her glumly.

'We'll see once it's all cleaned up.'

Natalie finished off and went to fetch Trish, who decided that the cut wasn't deep enough to warrant stitching. Ryan looked relieved when Natalie explained that she would hold the cut together with steristrips until it healed. She gave his whole arm a good cleaning with antiseptic then carefully placed the steristrips over the wound and bandaged his arm.

'How does that feel? Not too tight, is it?'

'No. It's OK.' Ryan waggled his arm about and nodded. 'It feels a lot better, thanks.'

'You're welcome.' Natalie smiled at him as she opened the cubicle door. 'If you have any problems with it, come straight back and we'll take another look at it. In the meantime, I suggest you go and take a bath. Here, let me give you this card. You can use the facilities at this hostel. There won't be a charge and nobody will ask you any questions.'

Ryan took the card from her and hurried away. Natalie sighed as she watched him leaving, because she had about as much hope of him attending to his personal hygiene as she had of flying to the moon!

Trish must have overheard the conversation because she chuckled as she came out of the neighbouring cubicle.

'I think you're on a loser there, Natalie. Young Ryan doesn't seem too keen on water to me.'

'Tell me about it,' Natalie said wryly, holding her nose.

Trish laughed in sympathy. 'Hmm, he did pong, didn't he? Still, he seemed a nice enough kid—even thanked me, which doesn't often happen. That's a point in his favour.'

'It is, and, let's face it, the poor boy needs something going for him, doesn't he?'

Trish was still laughing as Natalie made her way to the front desk to fetch their next patient. They saw half a dozen minor injuries then it was time for Trish to leave. Piers was on duty again that night and he grinned when he saw Natalie, or, more specifically, what she was wearing.

'I know you agreed to relax the dress code, Nat, but maybe you've gone too far the other way now. From full evening dress to scrub suit in the space of a week seems a big step down to me.'

'That's because you're too young to understand the protocol in these matters.' Natalie patted his cheek. 'One should *never* make the underlings feel uncomfortable. It's just not done.'

'Woowee! Get her!' Piers declared when Helen came out of the office to see what was going on. 'Our Nat should audition as a replacement for Emily Post. She's certainly well up on what is and isn't done in high society.'

Helen sniffed. 'Our Nat, as you call her, could give Emily Post a run for her money without any difficulty. Do you have any idea who she actually is?'

'What do you mean?' Piers demanded, looking blank.

'Does the name Palmer Pharmaceuticals mean anything to you? I know you have a very limited knowledge of the big wide world but maybe you've heard them mentioned somewhere,' Helen said scathingly.

Natalie shifted uncomfortably. Although she had never tried to hide who she was, she hadn't made a song and dance about it either. She would hate to think that Piers might feel it necessary to treat her any differently once he found out who she was.

'Of course I've heard of Palmer's,' Piers retorted. 'Do you think I'm a complete moron...' He stopped and his jaw dropped as he stared at Natalie. 'You don't mean that our Nat is one of *those* Palmers, do you?'

'Got it in one. My, my, so there's at least one brain cell alive and well inside that head of yours.' Helen smiled beautifically as Piers spluttered. 'Easy now, sonny. Don't tax yourself too much. We don't want you doing yourself any permanent damage, do we, Natalie?'

'We certainly don't,' Natalie said briskly, deeming it time to bring the conversation to an end. Swinging round, she went to call in her next patient but didn't get very far because Piers suddenly dropped to his knees and proceeded to genuflect in front of her.

'Forgive me, oh, illustrious one. If I'd known who you were I would have shown suitable humility,' he intoned.

Natalie chuckled, because it was so typical of Piers to react this way. Her spirits lifted at the thought that nothing had changed as she gently jabbed him with her toe. 'You are forgiven this time but make sure you remember your place in future, slave.'

'Thank you, thank you, oh, mighty one. I am truly grateful.' He stood up, grinning widely as he made his way to Reception to fetch in another patient.

Natalie laughed as she glanced at Helen. 'A typical Piers reaction, wouldn't you say?'

'He's a complete idiot, isn't he?' the other nurse declared, although the warmth in her voice took the sting out of the comment.

'He is indeed, but his heart's in the right place and that's what matters most of all.'

Helen didn't say anything but Natalie saw her blush. She smiled to herself as she went out to Reception. It looked as though there might be a romance in the offing and it couldn't happen to two nicer people than Helen and Piers.

She sighed as she picked up the next patient's notes because she couldn't help wishing that her love life was as uncomplicated as theirs. Fat chance of that ever happening!

The queue of people waiting to be seen dwindled around ten o'clock so Natalie made a start on clearing up. She knew there would be another rush before they closed and it would help to have everything straight before then so she filed their notes and restocked the shelves in all the cubicles with dressings. She was just thinking about making herself a cup of coffee when the outer doors opened. She went to see who it was, gasping in dismay when she found Danny Kennedy clutching hold of the doorjamb.

'Piers, I need a hand out here!' she shouted, running over to the teenager. She looped his arm around her neck and managed to support him until Piers arrived to help her.

'Let's get him into a cubicle,' the young doctor said tersely, half carrying and half dragging the boy through Reception.

They got him onto a bed and Natalie whipped the oxygen mask off the wall and slipped it over his nose and mouth. Danny was struggling for breath, his lips blue-tinged from the lack of oxygen reaching his lungs.

'He's asthmatic,' she told Piers hurriedly. 'We've sorted out a treatment regime for him but there was a hiccup at the beginning of the week when someone stole his drugs. They broke one of his ribs in the process.'

'It could be a knock-on effect from that, I suppose, although it doesn't sound like an asthma attack to me,' Piers said worriedly, slotting the ends of his stethoscope into his ears. He listened to the boy's chest and shook his head. 'Something's not right. There's no crackling or wheezing sounds coming from his lungs—not much sound of anything, in fact. The airway could be completely blocked, of course, but I'm just not sure.'

'Shall I call an ambulance?' Natalie suggested. This wasn't the right time to worry about how Danny would react to a stay in hospital.

'Yes. I don't like the look of him at all.' Piers glanced round when Helen appeared. 'This kid needs to go to hospital a.s.a.p., if not sooner, so can you phone for an ambulance?'

'That's what I came to tell you. There's been a major incident at one of the stations and all the ambulances are busy with that,' Helen explained. 'Sam just phoned to warn us in case we had problems getting hold of one. He also said that all hospitals within the Central London area have closed their A and E departments until they know how many casualties they might be dealing with. All other emergency cases will be ferried out of the city.'

'That's just what we need!' Piers sounded really worried as he shot another look at the youngster. 'He needs urgent treatment and we can't afford to waste valuable time while he's driven around London. I don't have either the experience or the skill to know what to do for him.'

Natalie bit her lip. Danny was unconscious now and barely breathing, despite the oxygen he was receiving. He desperately needed to be seen by an experienced accident-and-emergency consultant, but it could take a while to get him to a hospital at the moment. Even though she hated the thought, she knew there was just one person who might be able to help them.

She quickly left the cubicle and went into the office. Rafferty picked up the receiver on the third ring and she shivered when she heard his deep voice flowing along the line. She really and truly didn't want to curry favour by telling him about the work she'd been doing at the clinic, but she had no choice when Danny's life could depend on it.

'It's me—Natalie,' she said without preamble. 'I need your help, Rafferty.'

'Where are you?'

There was no sign of panic in his voice yet she could hear the underlying urgency it held, and something warm and soft flowered inside her. Even if Rafferty didn't love her the way she wanted him to, he still cared.

'Brookside Clinic. Have you got a pen? I'll give you directions.'

She rattled out the instructions on how to get there and made him repeat them, because it was vital that he shouldn't get lost.

'OK, I've got that. I should be with you in about ten minutes, with a bit of luck,' he told her briskly. 'I've got my mobile phone with me so call me if you need to.'

'Will do.' She started to hang up then paused. 'Thank you,' she said softly, and heard him draw in a deep breath.

'You don't need to thank me. I'll always be here whenever you need me, Natalie.'

He didn't say anything else before he hung up. Natalie replaced the receiver, feeling her heart welling with a mix of emotions. She knew that he'd meant what'd he said, knew, too, that she could rely on him to help her. Rafferty would never let her down but did he love her as much as she loved him? Love her with every fibre of his being for the woman she was rather than the woman he wanted her to be?

She couldn't answer that question because only Rafferty knew the answer to it. All she could do was hope that someday he would be able to see beyond her background and focus on her, the woman who loved him with the whole of her heart. Maybe then he would realise just how precious love really was.

CHAPTER FIVE

RAFFERTY drove as fast as he could but the traffic was horrendous, so it took him almost fifteen minutes to reach the clinic. He parked his car outside and hurried across the pavement, taking stock as he went. He had no idea what Natalie was doing in a place like this, but the litter that was strewn across the pavement and the graffiti that covered the walls of the arches didn't bode well for what he would find inside.

It came as something of a shock, therefore, when he opened the door and found himself in a pleasantly appointed reception area with rows of seats neatly lined up against the walls. There was even a vase of flowers on the counter and a couple of good-quality prints on the white-painted walls, so it definitely wasn't what he'd been expecting, but there again Natalie had a way of tossing surprises at him, didn't she?

'Oh, am I glad to see you! Come straight through.'

All of a sudden Natalie was there and Rafferty forgot everything else when he saw the worry on her beautiful face. He hurriedly followed her through the door behind the reception desk, rapping out questions as he went.

'What's happened? Why did you phone me?'

'We have a sixteen-year-old male asthmatic. He presented at the start of the week with the usual symptoms you would expect to find in someone suffering a severe asthma attack.'

'Is he following a treatment regime?' Rafferty cut in, wanting to have all the facts before him so he knew what he was dealing with.

'Yes. He's been responding well to sodium cromoglycate. The number of attacks he's suffered recently have been reduced by roughly half,' she explained, opening the door of the nearest cubicle and ushering him inside.

Rafferty nodded to the young doctor standing beside the bed, although he didn't waste time on introductions. There would be time enough for the pleasantries later. 'If he's been responding well, why did he suffer an attack earlier in the week?' he asked, going straight to the bed.

The younger man offered him a stethoscope and he nodded his thanks as he took it from him then checked the patient's general condition, which was pretty grim. The boy's breathing was so shallow as to be almost non-existent, his pulse rate was right off the scale and when Rafferty listened to Danny's chest, he could hear very little—not a good sign at all.

'Someone stole his medication so he wasn't able to take it as per instructions,' Natalie told him flatly, moving to stand beside him so that she could hold the boy's hand.

Rafferty felt a little spurt of awareness shoot through him when he saw her slender fingers squeezing the teenager's hand. If touch alone could cure the boy, he should be leaping off that bed by now, he thought wistfully. *He'd* always found Natalie's touch to be pure magic.

He hastily blanked out that thought because it wasn't the right time to start thinking about things like that. 'I see.' Looping the stethoscope around his neck, he unfastened the boy's shirt so he could examine him, frowning when he saw the discoloration all down the left side of his chest.

'How did this happen?' he demanded, shooting a look at Natalie.

'The people who stole Danny's medication also beat him up. I think he may have a cracked rib.'

'Has he been X-rayed?' Rafferty asked, gently feeling around the area. He tested Danny's upper abdomen and his frown deepened when he felt tension in the flesh beneath his fingertips.

'Danny refused to go to hospital.' She sighed when he looked at her in surprise. 'Like most of the kids we treat here, he's terrified of anything that smacks of authority. He stayed in the clinic on Monday night so I could keep an eye on him. He felt well enough to leave by lunchtime on Tuesday and I haven't seen him since then.'

Rafferty's brain was whirring as it started computing what he'd heard, not just the facts about young Danny but all the rest as well. Natalie had kept Danny in the clinic on Monday night? But Monday had been the night they'd attended that dinner, the same night that she'd run out on him to—presumably—visit her boyfriend? Either she'd packed an awful lot into Monday night or he'd been mistaken about the boyfriend.

The thought sent his spirits soaring and he had to make a determined effort not to start grinning like a Cheshire cat. He cleared his throat as he turned to the younger doctor, falling back on professional matters because it was so much safer.

'Any ideas what might be wrong with him?'

'None at all. That's why I told Nat I needed help.'

There was a refreshing lack of bravado about his answer which Rafferty appreciated. In his experience, it was rare to find a newly qualified doctor willing to admit that he didn't know everything about medicine, and Rafferty said so.

'Good to hear that you're willing to learn. You'll go far with that attitude.'

He turned to Natalie again because he didn't expect an answer and was pleased when the younger man didn't give him one. Trying to thank him for the compliment would have ruined the favourable impression the younger man had made. 'I'm going to need a scalpel, a catheter, a tube and a bottle.'

'You think Danny's suffering from a haemothorax!'

Rafferty smiled. It was typical of her to latch on so quickly to his train of thought. It was what made her such a superb nurse and his determination to get her back into the field on a full-time basis increased tenfold.

'Yes, I do. He's exhibiting all the classic signs—difficulty breathing, raised pulse rate, tenderness and tension in the upper abdomen. My guess is that the rib he cracked has been rubbing away at the lining of the pleural cavity and caused a slow bleed. The pleural space has been gradually filling up with blood and now his left lung has collapsed. We need to get it sorted out before the right one collapses as well.'

'I'll fetch what you need,' she said, hurrying away.

Rafferty turned back to the younger doctor. 'Let's get him positioned so I can get that tube in with the least amount of fuss. It's vital we get it done before his right lung packs up as well. I'm Michael Rafferty, by the way. I didn't get round to introducing myself before.'

'Piers Dutton,' the younger man replied, hurrying round the bed to help him. 'And I know who you are, sir, because I work at the same hospital as you, although I'm just a lowly second-year house officer.'

'We all have to start somewhere,' Rafferty replied laconically, positioning the patient flat on the bed because it would be easier to find the intercostal muscle—the sheets of muscle between the ribs which helped to expand and contract the chest during breathing—if the boy was lying down.

Natalie came back just then with what he needed, so he wasted no time after she'd swabbed an area below the teenager's left armpit. A quick incision through the flesh and muscle with the scalpel, then he was able to insert the catheter and attach it to a length of plastic tubing which led in turn into an empty bottle. Blood immediately began to gush into the bottle as the chest cavity emptied. One bottle quickly filled up so he replaced it with a second, pleased to see that the flow was diminishing. By the time it had been reduced to a trickle, Danny was breathing much easier and a short time later he regained consciousness.

'It's OK, Danny,' Natalie said soothingly, moving to the head of the bed. She took hold of the boy's hand and smiled at him. 'You had some blood in your chest that has been making it difficult for your lungs to work properly, but Dr Rafferty has sorted it all out now and you're going to be fine.'

Danny tried to speak but he was hampered by the oxygen mask so Rafferty moved it out of the way, trying not to breathe in too deeply because the fragrance of Natalie's perfume was having its usual effect on him. Ripples of pleasure danced across his nerves like a bow across violin strings and he had to force himself not to groan out loud in delight as he smiled at the teenager.

'You're going to feel a bit sore for a few days but you'll be fine, as Natalie said.'

'Will I have to go to hospital?' Danny asked fearfully, so fearfully, in fact, that Rafferty frowned.

'I'm afraid so. You're going to need time to heal, and going back on the streets in your present condition would be a very foolish thing to do.'

The boy's eyes filled with tears. 'The people at the hospital won't tell my mum, will they? I don't want her to know where I am in case *he* finds out. He said he'd kill me if he ever saw me again!'

Raffery glanced at Natalie for guidance, unsure who the boy was referring to, and she quickly drew him to one side.

'He means his mother's boyfriend. Apparently, he came to live with them after Danny's parents split up and he used to beat Danny up. That's why he ran away from home and ended up on the streets.'

Rafferty swore under his breath because it wasn't the first time he'd heard of something like that happening. Several of the children he'd been in care with had suffered the same fate, in fact, and he felt the same kind of anger and sense of injustice now that he'd felt then.

'Surely the police could have done something to help?' he snapped.

'Maybe they could have done but Danny was too afraid to tell them what had happened.' She sighed, obviously sensing his anger yet not fully understanding the reason for it. 'I know how you feel, Rafferty, but it was drummed into me before I started working here that I must never try to interfere. The kids who come to us for treatment will stop coming if they think we're working hand in glove with the authorities.'

'And that's the last thing you want,' he agreed flatly.

He made his way back to the bed, furious with himself for making it appear as though he'd been criticising her when he knew absolutely nothing about the work she was doing at the clinic. The thought stung, because he hated to feel as though she'd cut him out of her life and couldn't understand why she hadn't told him about the clinic. However, that was a question he would have to ask her at a later time, *after* he'd resolved this issue.

'I give you my word that your mother won't be contacted if that's what you want, Danny,' he told the boy firmly. 'I'll have you admitted to the hospital where I work so I'll be able to oversee your case myself. There's nothing to worry about, I promise you.'

Relief shone in the boy's eyes as he mumbled his thanks. Rafferty patted him on the shoulder then turned to Piers. 'Can you keep an eye on him for me, please? I need to arrange for an ambulance to transfer him to hospital.'

'Sure.' Piers looked starstruck as he studied Rafferty's handiwork. 'That was one of the most amazing things I've ever seen. Oh, I know the theory, of course, but I've never actually seen it put into practice before.'

'Well, you know what they say about practice making perfect,' he responded laconically, and Piers laughed.

'I could practise for years and never be as good a surgeon

as you are! You were a legend amongst the students in my year at my university. You're the reason I decided to become a surgeon, in fact. I read about the work you do with Worlds Together and was inspired.'

'It's a tough job but it's very fulfilling if you can stand the pressure,' he agreed soberly. 'We're always looking for volunteers to work with us so give me a call if you fancy doing a stint with one of our teams and I'll arrange an interview for you. Here's my home phone number if you prefer to get in touch outside working hours.'

Rafferty handed over his card as Piers stuttered his thanks. He headed for the door then paused and glanced back. 'And if surgery is your ultimate goal, I suggest you ask to be put on my team when it's time for your next rotation. The sooner you make a start on your training, the better.'

Piers was almost beside himself with delight as he and Natalie left the cubicle together. She looked at him and laughed.

'Spreading joy and happiness wherever you go, Rafferty? Although I don't know what use Piers is going to be to us for the rest of the night after this. He's going to find it very difficult to treat any patients while he's floating on cloud nine!'

Rafferty chuckled. 'Nice to know I can still have a positive effect on someone.'

Her brows rose. 'Meaning?'

He sighed because he hadn't realised how revealing the remark had been. However, now that the opening had presented itself, he might as well take advantage of it. 'Meaning that I don't seem to have been having much effect on you, Natalie. Not of a positive nature, anyway.'

'You're wrong there. I was very impressed by the way you diagnosed and treated Danny so quickly.'

'I wasn't talking about Danny.' He glanced around then led her into an empty cubicle and closed the door. Natalie walked over to the couch and sat down, looking rather strained as she waited for him to continue. Rafferty knew there wasn't an easy way to explain what he'd meant so he launched straight in.

'I was wrong to barge my way into your office the other day,' he admitted, knowing that he owed her an apology first for the way he'd behaved.

'You were,' she stated, and there was nothing in her voice to tell him if she was prepared to forgive him or not.

Rafferty forced himself to carry on but he could tell that it wasn't going to be easy to convince her that he had her best interests at heart. 'I was also wrong to say the things I did. The work you've been doing lately is important. I realise that now, although it doesn't alter the fact that I feel you're wasting your talents by working at Palmer's,' he said bluntly, hoping that he wasn't burning all his bridges by being completely honest with her.

He took a deep breath when she didn't reply then carried on because he might as well cut himself an even bigger slice of humble pie. 'I'm also sorry that I find it difficult to accept the fact that your family is so rich.'

'Why is it such a problem for you?' she interjected quietly.

'Because it makes me feel inadequate to know the kind of life you've led.'

'Inadequate? You?'

Rafferty smiled thinly when he heard the surprise in her voice. This was the most painful bit of all, yet he knew that they would never get anywhere if he wasn't truthful with her. He went and sat down beside her on the couch, feeling a ripple run through him when his arm brushed hers. He was always deeply aware of her, no matter what they were doing, and it made no difference that they were having a serious conversation because his body still responded to her closeness. The thought of her not wanting to continue their relationship once she found out the truth about him was almost too painful to contemplate, but he owed her an explanation.

'Yes, me. I've never had any of the material advantages you've enjoyed, Natalie. You see, I was brought up in care—passed from pillar to post between a succession of foster-homes after my mother abandoned me as a toddler.'

'It must have been hard for you, growing up like that, Rafferty,' she said softly, and his heart jolted painfully when he heard the compassion in her voice, because the last thing he wanted from her was sympathy. It all came back to the main sticking point in their relationship, the one that had always troubled him, about them being on an equal footing. He couldn't live with the thought that he might become an object of pity in her eyes.

'It wasn't easy but I survived,' he said brusquely. 'However, there's no point in me claiming that it hasn't left its mark because it's all too apparent at times. The way I was brought up means that I know nothing about your world and the people you mix with.'

He held up his hand when she started to protest because, now that he'd got this far, he didn't intend to stop. 'No, Natalie, it needs saying. You and I are worlds apart. Oh, I'm a first-rate surgeon and I'm not shy about admitting it either, but my education is lacking in so many respects that I won't even mention the areas I know very little about. Don't get me wrong: I don't have a chip on my shoulder, and I'm proud of what I've achieved, but I just don't think I'm the right man for you.'

Natalie felt as though someone had just punched her in the chest. How could Rafferty think that what he'd told her about his childhood would matter to her? Didn't he know that it was the person he was whom she loved: the brave, dedicated, clever surgeon; the tender, gentle lover. The rest meant absolutely nothing to her, although he obviously thought that it should. And it was the fact that he could misjudge her so badly that hurt most of all, because it hinted at a total lack of understanding about the person she was. If Rafferty didn't know that she wouldn't judge him by his background, there was no hope for them!

She stood up abruptly, too hurt to explain how devastated she felt. She didn't want to start an argument with him because it wasn't the right place. Anyway, what could she say when he'd already made up his mind?

'Natalie?'

Rafferty stood up as well and she could tell from his expression that he'd completely misconstrued her reaction. It was yet another damning indictment of how far apart they really were. If he'd loved her the way she loved him then he would have known without her having to tell him that she didn't give a damn about his background!

'I'm sorry but I really don't have time to discuss this,' she said shortly, opening the door.

'I apologise. Obviously my social skills are even worse than I imagined them to be.'

She rounded on him in fury at that. 'Don't you dare! You are not using that as an excuse. If you want to talk about this further, we'll do so, but don't try using your so-called lack of *social polish* as the reason why I don't wish to talk about it now!'

He had the grace to look discomfited but she wasn't prepared to continue the conversation. She left the cubicle and went to check on Danny, who was looking much better now. Piers was still with him but he excused himself once he knew she was staying because there were other patients waiting to be seen. Natalie made Danny comfortable then glanced round when the door opened and Rafferty appeared.

'There'll be an ambulance here in about five minutes' time to collect him,' he told her shortly, before he turned to the boy. 'I'll go with you to the hospital, Danny, and make sure there's no problems when you're checked in.'

Natalie bit her lip. She could tell from his tone that Rafferty was upset. It hurt to know that, yet there was very little she could do. How could he possibly believe that the way he'd been brought up would affect her feelings for him?

By the time the ambulance arrived, she'd worked herself into a state of righteous indignation and it didn't help when she discovered that he'd ordered a private ambulance to ferry Danny to the hospital. Had it reached the point whereby he thought that he had to impress her?

'You should have saved your money,' she hissed, *sotto voce*, as they accompanied Danny outside.

Rafferty immediately understood what she meant. 'I didn't hire it to improve my standing in your eyes, if that's what you think. It was a straight choice between getting a private ambulance to take Danny to hospital or waiting for an NHS one to ferry him to the suburbs. There's a major incident on in the city, in case you've forgotten.'

'Oh! I see.' She had forgotten, of course, but she wouldn't give him the satisfaction of admitting it. She waited in silence while the crew loaded the boy on board.

Rafferty unlocked his car then turned to look at her and she could see the chill in his eyes. 'I'll be staying on at the hospital to help so you can contact me there if you need to.'

'I won't,' she snapped.

'Fine. Then I'll see you on Monday morning, I expect.'

He got into the car and slammed the door. Natalie watched as he set off after the ambulance, very much aware that she'd handled the situation badly. There'd been no need to snap at him like that but she hadn't been able to stop herself after those crass remarks he'd made.

She stormed back into the clinic, almost flattening poor Helen who happened to be standing on the other side of the door when she flung it open. 'Sorry,' she muttered, feeling herself flush when she saw the knowing look her friend was giving her.

'So he's the one, is he?'

'Who's the one what?' Natalie replied with scant regard for any of the rules of grammar that she'd been taught at her expensive boarding school.

'The guy who thought he was on a promise the other night when he saw you in that fab dress.' Helen grinned. 'I see what you meant then about him spitting tacks. I have to say that his expression was less than sweet when he left just now.'

'It was, wasn't it?' Natalie laughed, her bad temper suddenly fizzling out. 'We had a bit of a disagreement, I'm afraid.'

'Tell me something I don't know!'

Helen rolled expressive dark eyes as she linked her arm through Natalie's and led her into the office. There was a pot of coffee on the hob so she filled a couple of mugs and plonked them on the desk. 'Come on—sit down and tell your Auntie Helen all about it.'

'You don't want to know.' Natalie subsided into a chair. She took a gulp of coffee and grimaced. 'That's disgusting! How long has it been stewing in the pot?'

'I've no idea. Stop complaining and just get it down you,' Helen replied unsympathetically. 'Now, you were saying about the gorgeous Dr Rafferty…?'

'Handsome is as handsome does.' Natalie glowered, burying her nose in the mug. 'He is the most pig-headed, the most infuriating, the most…most…'

'Mmm, but you love him, don't you?' Helen said smugly.

'Yes, I do. More's the pity!' She abandoned the mug and stood up, too on edge to sit still while her emotions were in such a turmoil. 'Rafferty has a problem with my family, you see, or, more specifically, the fact that they are so wealthy.

He can't seem to get past that fact and that's why we've always argued so much.'

'And is it still the major issue?' Helen asked astutely.

'It's never been an issue as far as I'm concerned,' Natalie replied loftily, then sighed because it was pointless taking the moral high ground. 'Not really. I'm just not sure if he loves me as much as I love him. If he did then the money or our backgrounds wouldn't matter. It also wouldn't matter that I'm working at Palmer's instead of nursing full-time. Real love should be able to transcend silly and irrelevant things like that.'

'If only.' Helen's tone was tinged with sadness and Natalie looked at her in surprise.

'You've been in the same situation?'

'Similar.' Helen made a brave attempt to smile. 'Not that it was my family's wealth that got in the way, you understand. We're just your average middle-class family so that was never an issue. However, the colour of my skin was. I was engaged, you see, only my fiancé's parents couldn't accept the fact that my mother is black. In the end we split up because of the problems it was causing between us.'

'I am *so* sorry!' Natalie sat down again, wishing there was something more she could say.

'Oh, I'm over it now, but it's made me very wary about getting involved with anyone else.'

'I've always been wary of relationships,' Natalie confessed. 'I was never sure if a man was interested in me or my family's money.'

'But Rafferty doesn't give a damn about your money,' Helen protested.

'No, he doesn't. But does he really love me for myself? That's something I just don't know for sure.'

'Then you should ask him, make him tell you how he feels and be honest about your fears.' Helen leant forward. 'You love the guy, Natalie, so are you going to behave like a wimp and just throw in the towel?'

'No. You're right. I should talk to him…' She broke off and sighed. 'Although talking has never been our strong suit, I have to say.'

'I'm not even going to ask what was,' Helen replied drolly. 'But I'm sure there's a way around this, if you can only find it and if you want it enough.'

'Yet there wasn't a way round your problem,' Natalie pointed out, and Helen shrugged.

'No, because Jack—that was his name—didn't love me enough to stand his ground. That's why I called off the engagement—because he simply didn't love me enough to fight for me.'

'And what if it's the same for me?' Natalie asked huskily. 'What if Rafferty doesn't love me enough to overcome his prejudices?'

'I don't know, love. But surely it would be better to find out, one way or the other, wouldn't it?'

Helen gave her a hug then left the office. A few moments later Natalie heard a commotion outside. It seemed that a gang of drunks had decided to invade the clinic so she went out to help clear the place. By the time that was done, the last-minute rush had started and there wasn't time to draw breath as they attended to their patients. It was well past midnight when they finally shut for the night.

Piers was going on to a club to meet some friends and didn't need a lift, so Natalie was on her own in the taxi. She was halfway home when it struck her that she wouldn't be able to rest with the memory of what had happened between her and Rafferty hanging over her. She tapped on the glass and asked the driver to take her to the hospital, then spent the rest of the journey perched on the edge of her seat, wondering what she was going to say when she saw him. Helen was right. She did need to ask him how he felt about her—but she was scared of what he might say.

By the time the cab drew up outside the hospital, she had worked herself into a real panic. She paid the fare and went inside, explaining to the receptionist that she needed to see Dr Rafferty. The woman made several phone calls and finally tracked him down to the surgical ward, so Natalie made her way up to the third floor.

She stepped out of the lift and paused to get her bearings, glancing round when she heard voices coming from further along the corridor. She didn't want to disturb the patients by going into the ward so she followed the sound and stopped when she came to the office. The door was open so it wasn't as though she was deliberately eavesdropping because she couldn't help overhearing what was being said.

'Kids like the Kennedy boy bring trouble on themselves,' a male voice said witheringly. 'If he'd stayed at home with his family, this wouldn't have happened and we wouldn't be having to waste valuable time and resources treating him.'

Natalie gasped at the insensitivity of the comment. However, before she could say anything in Danny's defence, someone else spoke and she froze when she recognised Rafferty's voice.

'So you don't reckon that kids like Danny Kennedy deserve the same standard of care that everyone else receives in this hospital?'

Natalie shivered when she heard the icy note in his voice. She could tell that he was furiously angry and the other man must have realised it, too, because he sounded far less assured this time when he replied.

'I...ah...I just think it would be easier if the authorities rounded up these kids who live rough and sent them back to their parents. It would certainly make life easier for us.'

'And that's your main concern is it, Dr Jeffries—to have an easy life? It doesn't bother you that kids like Danny

Kennedy could be sent back to homes where they were being abused? So long as we get them out of our hair, then who cares what happens to them?'

'N-no. N-not when you put it like that, sir,' the younger man stammered.

'What other way is there to put it? Let's not beat about the bush, Dr Jeffries. These kids are a nuisance, aren't they? They clutter up our wards and cause chaos when it comes to our statistics. After all, they aren't on any of our lists, so why should we waste our time on them when we could use it to treat more worthy patients?'

'Oh, I wouldn't go that far, sir!' The younger doctor affected a nervous laugh, obviously hoping to defuse the situation. However, Rafferty was relentless as he continued. Natalie shivered. Despite their many disagreements, she'd never heard him speak to anyone that way before. Once again she was struck by the thought that there was a side to him she knew nothing about.

'Wouldn't you? That's good to hear. But let me make myself perfectly clear, Dr Jeffries. Every single patient in this ward will be treated with the respect they deserve, and that includes Danny Kennedy or any other youngster who has been living on the streets. It might surprise you to learn that I've witnessed at first hand what happens to kids like Danny, and it isn't pleasant. So the next time you feel it necessary to prove your superiority by talking down to a patient, I suggest you think about whether or not you wish to remain a member of this team.'

'Yes, sir. Sorry, sir. Thank you.'

Natalie stepped aside as the younger doctor came rushing out of the office. He was so intent on making his escape that he didn't notice her standing there. Despite what he'd said about poor Danny, she could sympathise with him in a way, because she wouldn't have wanted to be on the receiving end of that dressing-down either.

She looked up when Rafferty suddenly appeared. He stopped when he saw her and she watched a dozen different emotions cross his face in swift succession. She had no idea if he was pleased to see her or not, but she knew that one of them had to try and resolve this problem otherwise it would only get worse.

'Sounded as though you were laying down the law,' she said lightly, feeling her way with care.

'I will not tolerate members of my staff patronising any patient on this ward,' he said sharply, closing the door.

'So I gathered.' She cleared her throat. 'How's Danny doing?'

'As well as can be expected in the circumstances.' He turned to look at her. 'So did you come here just to ask after Danny or was there another reason for your visit?'

'I wanted to talk to you, Rafferty. We need to sort out a few things—' She broke off when a nurse suddenly appeared.

Rafferty waited until the woman had passed them before he said brusquely, 'I think we said everything that needed saying before.'

'No, we didn't. We never do because we always end up at cross purposes—'

Once again she had to break off when the same nurse reappeared, carrying a bundle of sheets this time. Rafferty shook his head when she attempted to carry on after the nurse had gone back inside the ward.

'We can't talk here. There's people coming and going along this corridor all the time and I, for one, don't want my private life to become the latest topic of gossip.' Digging in his pocket, he took out his car keys and handed them to her. 'Wait in the car for me. I just need a word with the ward sister then I'm going home. We can talk back at my flat.'

Natalie took the keys without demur and headed for the lift. There was no point refusing to go back to his flat, because they needed to sort this out sooner rather than later.

Within a few minutes she was in the underground parking lot and heading for Rafferty's car, which was parked in a consultant's bay.

Unlocking the door, she got in, feeling her heart pounding as she settled down to wait for him. Even though she knew they needed to talk about their problems, she wasn't confident about the outcome—even less so after what she'd overheard just now. It wasn't just Rafferty's reaction that bothered her, however. It was what he'd said about having witnessed the harm that could befall youngsters like Danny Kennedy. If she added that to what he'd told her earlier that night about his own childhood, it made her see just how different his life had been to hers, and how hard it would be to convince him that it didn't matter.

Would they be able to find some common ground to talk about the problems it seemed to be causing between them? she wondered anxiously, but it was a question she couldn't answer. It would all depend on how receptive Rafferty was to what she had to say. All she could do was hope that she could convince him that his past didn't matter. If she couldn't, she didn't know what they were going to do.

Panic suddenly rushed through her and her hands clenched as she realised she simply couldn't imagine living the rest of her life without him.

CHAPTER SIX

RAFFERTY unlocked the front door of his flat and stepped aside so Natalie could precede him inside. He had no idea what she'd hoped to achieve by coming to see him that night. By tacit consent neither of them had said anything on the drive home. However, he knew that no matter how difficult this meeting might turn out to be, he couldn't have sent her away. He loved her too much and if she needed him in any way, shape or form, he would always be there for her.

'I hope you weren't planning on going straight to bed when you got in.'

He looked round when she spoke, feeling the same mixture of pain and pleasure he always seemed to feel of late whenever they were together. She was so precious to him that he longed to take her in his arms and hold her—just hold her—until all their problems disappeared. Unfortunately, life wasn't that simple and these problems they faced weren't just going to magically vanish.

'Actually, I was going to have a drink before I turn in for the night.' He led the way to the kitchen and took a bottle of white wine out of the refrigerator. 'Care to join me?'

'Why not?'

Natalie took a couple of glasses off the shelf and followed him into the sitting room. She put them on the table then sat down on the couch and waited while he opened the bottle. Rafferty filled the glasses with wine and handed her one before he sat down in the chair opposite her.

'Mmm, this is rather nice.' She took another sip of the wine then reached for the bottle and studied the label. 'I wonder if it's the same one Dad ordered from his wine merchant last month. It tastes very similar, I must say.'

'I doubt it.' Rafferty laughed shortly as he swung his feet onto the coffee-table. 'As it cost a mere four pounds ninety-nine from the local supermarket, I doubt if it's the same exhalted vintage.'

Her face closed up as she put the bottle back on the table. 'You never miss an opportunity, do you, Rafferty? You're determined to keep highlighting the differences between us, even if it's only through the cost of a bottle of wine. If it weren't so petty, it would be laughable!'

Rafferty took a sip of wine, not that he could taste it properly. Sour grapes had their own particular flavour and his comment had smacked very strongly of that. 'I'm sorry,' he said brusquely. It seemed as though he'd done nothing but apologise that night.

Natalie shrugged, not even deigning to say whether or not she'd forgiven him, although probably she hadn't. The thought stung and he glowered as he raised the glass to his lips once more. He was willing to meet her halfway but he wasn't willing to fall at her feet and beg her forgiveness if that's what she expected from him.

They sat in silence while the minutes ticked past. Rafferty knew it was ridiculous to play this kind of childish game but he refused to give in. When she plonked her glass on the table and stood up, he just looked at her.

'There's no point in me being here if we aren't going to talk.'

'I'm happy to listen to anything you have to say,' he stated coolly, swirling the wine around his glass.

'That's very good of you. You're willing to listen but you're not willing to make the first move?'

He shrugged, wondering if she realised how beautiful she looked when she got all steamed up like that. His body made a sudden very positive statement to let him know that *it* had noticed how lovely she was, and he hastily crossed his legs. The last thing he wanted was for her to know the power she had over him. So maybe he did want to drag her off to bed and make mad, passionate love to her but he wasn't going to give in to the urge…

Just yet.

The thought of sexual fulfillment was just too much and he shot to his feet. Picking up the bottle, he refilled their glasses then gestured to the sofa. 'Why don't you sit down and we can start again? Then you can tell me why you wanted to see me.'

Her eyes narrowed as she weighed up his invitation, obviously testing it out to see if it had been a genuine attempt to resolve the issue. It must have passed muster because she suddenly sat down again and picked up her glass.

Rafferty resumed his own seat, although he left his glass on the table. He didn't intend to cloud his head with alcohol until he found out exactly what she wanted from him.

'Were there any problems about Danny being admitted?'

It was Natalie who made the opening gambit and he responded in kind, his pawn meeting hers on neutral ground.

'No. As I have no idea where he used to live, there was no way that I could have informed his mother that he was in hospital. The social worker will visit him tomorrow but I've left a note on his file to ask her to contact me before she does anything.'

'Good. The last thing poor Danny needs is to start worrying about his stepfather finding him.'

She took another sip of her wine then fell silent, apparently having exhausted the only safe topic of conversation she could think of. Despite his earlier reluctance to take the lead, Rafferty realised that he wanted to keep the lines of communication open. They would get nowhere if they didn't talk to one another and it was up to him to do his bit now.

'So how did you get on at the clinic after I left?' he asked, opting for another safe topic. He sighed under his breath. It was ridiculous to keep skirting around the reason why she'd come to see him that night. He should just ask her, point-blank, why she'd needed to speak to him so urgently, although he couldn't pretend that he wasn't worried about what she might say. Maybe it would be safer to wait until she was ready to broach the subject rather than press her. 'Was it very busy?'

'Bedlam. Mind you, it didn't help when we were invaded by some drunken yobs whose sole aim, it seemed, was to cause as much mayhem as possible. By the time we'd got rid of them, there was a queue of people all round Reception, waiting to be seen.'

'Did you call the police to deal with the drunks?' he demanded, hating to think of her having to deal with a situation like that.

'No. We don't call in the police as a rule because they only scare away the very people we're trying to help. A lot of the kids we treat at the clinic have been in trouble with the police and they're terrified of being locked up again.'

'But surely it's dangerous to work there without any kind of back-up. Couldn't you at least hire a private security firm to guard the clinic and prevent that kind of thing happening?'

'There simply isn't enough money in the budget to pay for it. We have a hard enough time covering our costs as it is.' She shrugged. 'We manage, Rafferty. OK, so it can get a bit hairy at times but there's not been a really serious incident there since the clinic opened last year.'

'I'd still feel happier if I knew there was somebody around you could call on in case of any trouble,' he persisted.

'I'm a grown woman and I can take care of myself. And it's not as though I haven't had experience of working in dangerous places, is it?' she pointed out reasonably enough.

'No. But whenever we've been away on a mission there've

been other people around who could have helped you if the need had arisen.'

'The same as at the clinic. The staff there are great and we all work together as a team and help one another.'

Rafferty struggled to contain his frustration. It was obvious that she wasn't going to listen to his concerns and he didn't want to start another argument with her. 'How did you start working there in the first place?' he asked, switching to a less volatile subject.

'I read an article about the clinic in one of the Sunday papers so I went along the following week and volunteered.'

'I see. Why didn't you tell me what you were doing? You could have told me on Monday night when you had to leave that dinner so suddenly, but you refused to say where you were going. Why did you decide to keep it a secret?'

'Because I didn't want you to know.'

'Why on earth not?' He couldn't hide his surprise and he saw her flush.

'Because I didn't want you to think that I was trying to curry favour with you.'

'Curry favour,' he repeated blankly.

'Yes! You've made no bones about the fact that you think I've been wasting my time in London so why should I try to improve your opinion of me?'

She shot to her feet again, almost dropping her glass in the process. Rafferty stood up and took it from her but his heart was hammering all of a sudden. He had a horrible feeling that they were getting to the reason why she'd sought him out that night and he was terrified that he might say or do the wrong thing.

'You don't need to improve anything for my sake,' he said softly, but with so much emotion that it actually hurt to force the words out of his mouth.

'Don't I? So you love me as I am and it doesn't matter if I'm a nurse or the acting head of Palmer's?' She tipped back her head and stared him straight in the eyes, and the pain inside him seemed to double in intensity. He hadn't realised that he'd hurt her so deeply and he couldn't bear to think of the damage he must have caused.

'I only want what is best for you, Natalie,' he said, each word demanding such an effort that he felt quite weak. He had to make her believe him, but did she? 'That's all I've ever wanted.'

'And what if I don't think it *is* the best thing for me? What if my ideas differ from yours? What happens then, Rafferty?'

'I don't know!' he exploded as his frustration spilled over. He'd told her the truth, yet even that wasn't enough, it seemed. 'I've explained my reasons and I don't understand what else you expect me to say!'

'No. Obviously not.'

All of a sudden the fight seemed to drain out of her and his heart contracted with fear when he saw how bereft she looked. Reaching out, he pulled her into his arms and kissed her, wanting—*needing*—to bring back the feisty Natalie he loved more than life itself. Her mouth was passive under his at first, neither responding nor fighting, and his fear intensified. Somehow, some way, he had to break through this barrier she was erecting between them!

His lips plundered hers again, teasing, tasting, caressing in the most erotic way he knew, and gradually he felt a glimmer of a response. Buoyed up by his success, he trailed more kisses across her cheek and along her jaw, nibbling the warm skin on her throat and glorying in the little murmur she gave in response. When her hands moved up to rest on his shoulders he could have shouted for joy—only his mouth was far too busy with more important matters.

His lips skimmed down her throat and along her collarbone this time and he felt her shudder. She was wearing a white silk blouse with a deep V-neckline and it was easy-peasy to skate his lips down one slope of the V and back up the other.

'Rafferty.'

His name was no louder than the faintest whisper in the depths of the night but he heard it and it was enough to encourage him to keep going. He *could* get through to her, if he tried hard enough!

His hands glided up from her waist to brush the undersides of her breasts and he felt her suck in her breath, heard the sudden intake of breath he took as well. Sensations were rippling through him but he made himself focus on her needs rather than his own. It was Natalie who mattered most and he had to convince her not to shut him out but to keep all lines of communication between them wide open.

His hands glided over her breasts, his palms making the lightest contact imaginable with her nipples, but even so he felt them harden. She'd always been so sweetly responsive to his love-making in the past and his heart soared because it appeared that nothing had changed in that respect.

The thought filled him with joy as he kissed her with a hunger that left them both fighting for breath when he drew back. Her lips were red and swollen from his kisses, her eyes hazy with passion, and Rafferty knew that if they carried on they were going to reach the most natural of all conclusions. Whilst it was what he wanted with every fibre of his being, she had to want it, too—want it with her mind as well as her body.

He took a deep breath and stepped back, and every inch he put between them felt like a mile. He longed to be right back where he'd been just moments before—with Natalie in his arms and her heart beating in time with his—but he would never forgive himself if he used the passion they'd always felt for each other to persuade her to do something she could ultimately regret.

'Rafferty?'

She sounded bewildered by the speed with which he'd ended their love-making and his heart ached because if circumstances had been different, he wouldn't have had to stop. He would have swept her into his arms, carried her to his bed and then…

He blanked out the rest of the scene that was unfolding inside his head, because he wasn't strong enough to resist if he thought about what he was giving up.

'It might be better if we call a halt before things get too fraught,' he said quietly. Fraught was the perfect word, too, he thought grimly, because their love-making had been very *fraught* in the past. They had put their hearts and their souls into it but the result had been worth it. And it didn't make it any easier to behave sensibly when his head was awash with such delectable memories.

'I see.'

Natalie made an obvious effort to collect herself and his hands clenched, because it was hard to stand there and watch her struggling for control when he was the one who had caused her to lose it in the first place. Flicking back her hair, she stood up straighter and he bit back a sigh when he saw that her composure was rapidly returning. Although he loved her in every way it was possible to love another person, he couldn't deny that his love was at its most intense when she was soft and pliant in his arms.

He knew exactly what to do then but it was far more difficult to know how to respond when she slipped back into this other persona—the beautiful, sophisticated woman-about-town. It just seemed to highlight his fears that he could never live up to her expectations and it was galling to have such doubts when he wasn't a person who normally had reservations about his own ability. He was proud of what he'd achieved in his life, confident of his skills as a surgeon, yet he was afraid that he could never measure up to the kind of man whom Natalie needed to make her happy. And it was that fear, lingering at the back of his mind, which was causing the damage.

'I think I'd better go, don't you?' She picked up her bag and went to the door.

Rafferty followed her with his heart bouncing somewhere around his feet. He knew that many men would have swept aside their misgivings and concentrated on the moment instead of worrying about the future, but he wasn't like them. His feelings for Natalie weren't like that either, because he didn't want an affair with her. He wanted the whole works: marriage and a family; the happily-ever-after that followed the ride off into the sunset. He wanted her by his side and in his heart until the day he died.

But did she want him like that, for ever and always, until death did them part?

Maybe she enjoyed having sex with him, even loved him in her own way, but she might grow tired of being with a man who wasn't her social equal, or of the constant problems that it would cause between them. And it was that idea that scared him most of all—the thought of having her today and losing her tomorrow. He didn't think he could bear it if that happened.

He took a deep breath but there was no way he could close his mind to the truth any longer. It might be better to let her go now than inevitably suffer the heartache of losing her at some point in the future.

Natalie wasn't sure what was going through Rafferty's mind but she could tell how abstracted he was as he saw her to the door. Maybe it had been a mistake to let him kiss her like that but in all honesty she couldn't claim that she hadn't wanted it to happen. It had been months since he'd held her in his arms and she hadn't realised just how much she'd missed the contact with him until tonight. If Rafferty hadn't called a halt then she certainly wouldn't have done and the thought seemed to awake all her earlier fears. If Rafferty loved her as much as she loved him, how could he have stopped just now?

The thought sent her spirits plummeting so that it was an effort to disguise how low she felt. 'Thank you for the wine,' she said politely. 'I hope I haven't kept you up too late?'

'Don't worry about it. I needed to unwind otherwise I won't be able to sleep tonight.'

His tone matched hers and she bit back a sigh. They were both behaving like guests at a vicarage tea party. However, the alternative—putting her arms around him and begging him to take her to his bed—was out of the question. Until she knew how Rafferty really felt about her, it would be better to avoid any more physical contact with him.

Her spirits, already low, sank the last few inches into the mire but it would be stupid to buoy them up with false promises. Sex had to be off the agenda until she knew if Rafferty loved her as much as she loved him, and that was all there was to it. She picked up the conversation again, falling back on work because it was always the safest topic, the one they never argued about.

'Were there many casualties from that incident tonight, by the way? I didn't have time to watch the news because we were so busy at the clinic so I don't even know what happened.'

'Turned out that it was a false alarm. Apparently, some people were waiting in one of the tube stations when they saw a man spraying something into the air and they assumed he was letting off toxic gas.' He grimaced. 'Everyone panicked and several dozen people were injured in the rush to get up the escalators.'

'How awful! If it was a false alarm, I assume he wasn't spraying anything harmful into the air.'

'It was perfume.' Rafferty shrugged when she gasped. 'Evidently, he'd bought some perfume for his wife and he decided to test it to make sure he'd got the right one. It must have been a shock for him when the police arrived and arrested him.'

'Oh, dear.' Natalie smiled wryly. 'His good intentions certainly went astray, didn't they?'

'They did, indeed.' He smiled rather grimly. 'The road to hell is paved with good intentions, though, don't they say?'

Natalie had no idea what to say to that so she let the comment pass. However, as she stepped into the lift a few minutes later, she couldn't help wondering if the remark had been based on personal experience. Had Rafferty's good intentions led him along a route he now wished he hadn't chosen?

A wave of sadness swept over her. She couldn't help wondering if maybe he regretted getting involved with her. Their relationship had been peppered with problems, and she couldn't blame him if he was tired of the constant arguments. She was tired of them, too, and desperately wanted to find a solution, but was it possible to resolve the issues that lay between them?

She'd gained a new insight into Rafferty's past today and even though it hadn't changed how she felt about him, she did understand now why he'd always felt so uncomfortable about her family's wealth. His childhood had left its mark on him just as hers had left its mark on her, and she had to accept that he might never come to terms with the difference in their backgrounds.

She didn't want to hurt him and certainly didn't want to put him under any more pressure. Rafferty had been through enough while he'd been growing up and it was a measure of the man he was that he'd made a success of his life after such an inauspicious start. She hated to think that she was the cause of these doubts he had so maybe it would be better if they stopped seeing each other. Even though she couldn't bear the thought of losing him, she had to face the fact that it might be the only solution.

A burst of laughter came from the neighbouring cubicle and Natalie paused. It was Sunday afternoon and she was working another extra shift at the clinic. Saturday had been a complete nightmare, as she'd been unable to rid herself of the thought that it might be better if their on-off relationship ended for good. After a sleepless night she'd realised that she had to stop brooding about it so she'd come into the clinic.

It had been a shock when she'd opened the door and seen Rafferty. He'd been talking to Helen and, from the look of it, they had been getting along famously, too. When Helen had called her over and told her that Rafferty had signed on as a volunteer, Natalie hadn't known what to say. She could hardly have objected to him working there when they were in desperate need of extra staff so in the end she'd murmured something about it being useful to have another experienced doctor on the team and left it at that. However, she still hadn't decided how she really felt about the idea. Would it be a good thing to spend more time with him when their relationship was at an all-time low?

'So what do you think's wrong with me, then? Every time I need to pee it burns like mad!'

Natalie hurriedly returned her attention to the girl sitting on the couch. Jade Baxter was sixteen and had been living in one of the local hostels. She had come to London six months ago after running away from the latest in a series of foster-homes. Of mixed Asian and Afro-Caribbean heritage, she was a strikingly pretty girl with curly black hair and huge dark brown eyes. Natalie had seen her several times since she'd been working at the clinic, each time over something fairly trivial. She suspected that Jade was lonely and that she came to the clinic to talk to them. However, there was no doubt that she was genuinely ill that day.

'I think you have cystitis, Jade. Your symptoms certainly point towards it—a frequent desire to urinate, pain accompanied by a burning sensation when you do manage to pee. Have you noticed any traces of blood in your urine?'

'No. Should I have done?' Jade asked anxiously, and Natalie smiled.

'No. It's just another symptom that would point towards it being cystitis. If you can give me a urine sample, I'll get it tested, although I'm ninety-nine per cent certain that's what is wrong with you.'

'But how did I get it? I mean, I've never had it before so why has it suddenly happened now?'

'There are all sorts of reasons,' Natalie explained, sitting down beside her on the couch. 'Cystitis occurs when the inner lining of the bladder becomes inflamed, usually because of a bacterial infection. Anything that stops you passing water can cause the infection because bacteria soon grow in stagnant urine. That's why it's so important to go to the loo as soon as you feel that you need to do so and not hang on until later.'

'Oh.' Jade pulled a face. 'I hate using the toilets at the hostel. The staff do their best but some people leave them in the most awful state. I tend to wait until I go to the shops then use the toilets in one of the big stores.'

'That's probably what's caused it, then. Constantly retaining urine in the bladder or the urethra—that's the tube leading out of your body—is providing the perfect breeding ground for all those nasty little bugs. You're going to have to bite the bullet and use the facilities at the hostel, I'm afraid. Maybe you could ask the staff if they would put up a notice, asking people to be more considerate.'

'I can try,' Jade said glumly, 'but I don't suppose it will do much good. Some people are absolutely disgusting!'

Natalie laughed sympathetically. 'Then you'll have to see about getting a place of your own. Have you contacted that housing association I told you about the last time you were here?'

'Yes. They were very nice but they explained that they have a huge waiting list so I don't know how long it will be before they can offer me a flat of my own.'

'That's a pity. What about the private sector? Have you tried that?' Natalie asked, getting up to unlock the cupboard and take out a prescription pad. She tore off a script and replaced the pad on the shelf then locked the cupboard again. Blank prescriptions were like gold dust and they had to be very careful that none of their patients could get hold of them, otherwise they might use them to obtain hard drugs. Being constantly on her guard about such matters was one aspect of the job which she'd had to adjust to, but now it was second nature to be careful.

'It's just too expensive to rent privately.' Jade sighed. 'The going rate for even a studio flat in London is way out of my league, even though I've just got myself a job.'

'Really?' Natalie exclaimed in delight. 'Where are you working?'

'Oh, just in a florist's shop not far from here. The money is rubbish but they've offered to train me so it's a start. And who knows? Maybe one day I can get my own shop.'

'Well, good for you! Everyone has to start somewhere and you never know where you'll end up in a few years' time.'

Natalie filled in the prescription and signed it, then handed it to the girl. As a qualified nurse-practitioner, there were a range of drugs she could prescribe without needing a doctor's signature on the prescription and this was one of them. 'Take this to the chemist along the road. The shop is open on Sundays and I'd like you to start taking the tablets as soon as possible.'

'What are they?' Jade asked, studying the script.

'Antibiotics. They will soon clear up the infection and everything should start to settle down within twenty-four hours or so. Make sure you finish the full course of tablets, though, because you don't want it coming back. And the other thing is to remember to drink plenty of fluids to flush out your bladder—plain water will do fine, or cranberry juice is very good if you can afford it.'

'It will have to be water,' Jade explained, standing up. 'I won't get paid until the end of the month so I'm broke. I can't afford to start buying fruit juice.'

'Water is just as good,' Natalie assured her, resisting the urge to offer the girl some money.

It was drummed into all the staff at the clinic that they must never give their patients any money. They were a medical facility, not a welfare centre. However, sometimes—like now, for instance—she found it very hard to stick to the rules. She had to content herself with the thought that she was working towards raising a sizeable donation for the clinic from Palmer's charitable fund, so that would help a number of their youngsters.

She saw Jade out and took her next patient through to the treatment area. That set the pattern for the rest of her shift and the time flew past. The evening staff came on duty at six so she cleared up and went to say hello to Sam Cummins, and found him talking to Rafferty. Helen was there as well and she beckoned Natalie over as soon as she appeared.

'It's been a really busy afternoon, hasn't it?' Helen declared, grinning at her. 'Good job we had two extra pairs of hands. Quite a coincidence you and Rafferty both turning up like that, wasn't it?'

'It was,' Natalie agreed, doing her best to ignore the meaningful looks Helen was giving her. Obviously, Helen was keen to find out if she and Rafferty had managed to resolve their differences but there was very little she could tell her when last night's chat had left her feeling more confused than ever.

'I was just saying to Rafferty that I didn't feel like going straight home tonight and he suggested that we all go out for a meal.' Helen looped her arm through Natalie's and steered her towards the door. 'Piers just phoned up to check when he's supposed to be working next week so I've invited him along as well. You're going to come with us, aren't you?'

'Oh, I don't think so,' Natalie began, but just then Rafferty came over to them.

'Has Helen told you that we're all going out for a meal?'

'Yes, she has,' Natalie replied coolly.

'Good. We fancied a curry so I hope that's all right with you. Helen said there's a restaurant not far from here which is very good.'

He seemed to have taken her agreement for granted as he followed them outside. Piers was coming along the street and Helen let go of her arm as she went to meet him. Natalie paused on the pavement, her eyes clouded with indecision as she turned to Rafferty.

'Do you really think it's a good idea for us to socialise like this?'

'We're only going for a curry, Natalie. Where's the harm in that?'

'None. But add it to the fact that you've suddenly decided to join the staff at the clinic and surely you can understand why I'm not exactly thrilled about the idea.'

'No, I can't, actually. OK, so maybe I should have let you know that I'd decided to volunteer to do a few shifts here, but I really didn't think it would be that much of a problem.'

'It isn't a problem,' she denied immediately, because she didn't want it to become a major issue.

'Good. So if it's the thought of us going out for a meal that's worrying you, I give you my word that I'm not planning anything else afterwards.'

'Afterwards?'

'Yes. I'm not about to try and get you into my bed, if that's what you're worried about. We already discussed that idea the other night. *And* decided it would be the wrong thing to do—remember?'

Natalie flushed. If last Friday night had proved anything, then it was how vulnerable she was where he was concerned, and it was a reminder she could have done without at that moment. 'I remember. However, we've let our emotions get the better of us far too often in the past and now I think it's time we really thought about what we intend to do.'

'Sounds like a sensible idea to me.'

Natalie frowned when she heard the grim note in his voice. It certainly didn't sound as though he believed it was the sensible option. 'I'm glad you agree,' she said firmly, determined not to let her resolve waver. She'd gone over this a thousand times and the more she'd thought about it, the more sense it had made. She just wasn't prepared to risk hurting him any more.

She took a quick breath and hurried on, because it would be easier for both of them if she got it over with as quickly as possible.

'I've given this a lot of thought, Rafferty, and I've decided that if we're never going to reach a compromise then I think we should end our relationship for good. It simply isn't worth putting ourselves through any more heartache.'

CHAPTER SEVEN

'I'LL have the chicken jalfrezi—extra hot—with naan bread.'

Rafferty gave the waiter his order and sat back in his seat, hoping the shock he was feeling wasn't apparent to everyone else. Hearing Natalie state that it might be better if they split up permanently had been a blow, even though he'd wondered if it might be the only solution open to them.

His gaze skimmed sideways and he felt his heart lurch once again. It was one thing to wonder about it himself, but something entirely different to know that she was considering such a course of action. Even though they'd split up before, they'd both known they would get back together at some point. But not this time. This time it would be different. Once the decision was made, that would be the end for them, and he didn't know how he was going to carry on without her.

'You're a brave soul!'

Rafferty jumped when Helen tapped him on the arm. He turned to face her, doing his best to behave as though everything was fine. It was a long way from being that—probably as bad as it could be, in fact—but he'd never been one for airing his feelings in public.

'Why do you say that?'

'Because you're going for the *extra*-hot jalfrezi. Only the very brave or the very foolhardy choose that option!'

Rafferty drummed up a smile when everyone laughed. 'I'll let you know which category I fall into after I've eaten it.'

Piers chuckled. 'I don't think there's much doubt about your bravery, sir. Not from what I've read about the work you've done overseas. Some of the places where you've been must have been very tough going.'

'They were. And cut out the "sir". Everyone calls me Rafferty.'

'Not all the time,' Natalie chipped in with a laugh.

Rafferty glanced at her, firmly squashing his heart back into its allotted place when it tried to leap out of his chest. So maybe she was smiling at him at the moment, but he couldn't take it as a good sign after what she'd told him. She was ready to cast him aside and a smile meant absolutely nothing in those circumstances.

'Meaning?' he asked, struggling for lightness and probably missing it by miles.

'*Meaning* that you have a nickname, don't you?'

She held his gaze for a moment then looked away, and he could tell by the tremor in her voice that she'd picked up the undercurrents. He sighed under his breath. He would have to do better than that if he hoped to convince her that he was unmoved by her decision to cut him out of her life. If she felt it was the right thing to do, he mustn't stand in her way…although it wasn't going to be easy to step aside.

'What nickname?' Piers demanded. 'I've never heard anyone mention it at the hospital.'

'It's only used when we're away on a mission,' Natalie explained. 'A lot of the people who work for Worlds Together have nicknames. Rafferty's is TC, which stands for Top Cat.'

Helen burst out laughing. 'I don't think I'll ask how he got it! Seems self-explanatory to me.'

Rafferty managed to smile but it wasn't easy to deal with all these emotions that were running riot inside him. 'I'm not sure if that was a compliment so I'm not going to comment.'

'Better not,' Helen replied cheerfully as she turned to Natalie. 'So what's your nickname, then? I take it that you do have one.'

'I do.' Natalie rolled her eyes. 'Hot-lips, would you believe?' She held up her hand when Helen opened her mouth.

'And before you ask, I have no idea why I got landed with it…apart from the fact that some of the folk who work for the agency have a very puerile sense of humour!'

Everyone laughed before the conversation moved on to a different topic. Rafferty joined in as best he could but it wasn't easy to appear upbeat when there seemed to be a dark cloud hanging over his head. Their meal arrived and the curry turned out to be just as hot as Helen had predicted it would be, but he ate the lot because it had been his decision to choose it.

That was the trouble with decisions, of course. Once they were made, it was difficult to *un*make them. If Natalie decided to call time on their relationship, he would have a hard job changing her mind, especially when he wasn't sure if it would be the right thing to do. Maybe she *would* be better off without him. Then she could find a guy who would fit into her life the way he would never be able to do.

Thoughts like that only served to make him feel even more depressed so that by the time they'd finished eating, Rafferty had reached an all-time low. When Piers suggested going on to a nightclub, he immediately declined.

'Sorry to be a party pooper but the only thing I'm fit for right now is bed.'

He stood up and smiled around the table, making sure his gaze didn't linger on Natalie because once it got stuck there it might never move on. 'I'll take care of the bill on my way out.' He shook his head when Piers started to protest. 'No, it's my treat so don't worry about it. Thanks for your company and enjoy the rest of your evening.'

Helen and Piers tried once more to persuade him to go with them but once again he declined. Natalie didn't say anything and he was very conscious of her silence as he said his goodbyes and went to pay the bill. There was a taxi dropping off a fare outside, so he got in and told the driver to take him home. And all the way there he kept thinking about him and Natalie splitting up. Was it the only option? He just didn't know.

Rafferty spent a sleepless night thinking about it so that by the time morning arrived the last thing he felt like doing was going in to Palmer's again that day. What was the point, anyway? Natalie seemed perfectly happy with what she was doing and it wasn't as though she had abandoned her nursing career altogether. She was working at the clinic, so surely he should be content with that. He should call a halt to this challenge he'd set her. After all, what right did he have to interfere in her life if she didn't want him to play any part in it?

It was a depressing thought and he found it hard to rid himself of an overwhelming sense of gloom as he got dressed and left the flat. Even though he hated the thought, he knew that he had to tell her his decision. Any plans he'd had about winning her back had to be forgotten, too. It would be best if they made a clean break, even though the thought of being without her made him feel ill. But it really didn't matter how he felt, did it? It was Natalie who mattered, her feelings his only concern. If she would be better off without him then he wasn't going to stand in her way.

He was just stepping out of the lift outside her office when his cellphone suddenly rang. Reaching into his pocket, he checked the display and frowned when he saw that it was Shiloh Smith, the head of Worlds Together, calling him. Veering off from the main corridor, he found a quiet spot near the window while he answered the call, his frown deepening when he heard what Shiloh had to say.

Five minutes later, Rafferty ended the call, wondering what he should do. Shiloh had told him that they were sending a team from Worlds Together to Honduras to assist in the aftermath of a hurricane that had swept through the country. Thousands of people had been left without food and shelter, and there were thousands more casualties. Rafferty hadn't hesitated as he'd agreed to head up the team, but it had left him in a bit of a quandary. He didn't want to leave until he'd talked to Natalie but what was he going to say to her? That he'd abandoned any hope of her returning to full-time nursing and that he was stepping aside so she could get on with her life? It was what he'd been planning on doing when he'd set out that morning, but all of a sudden he couldn't imagine telling her that. It would be too hard, too stressful, too…too *much*!

He took a deep breath as panic threatened to engulf him. He needed to think this all through and be sure about what he was going to do, because whatever decision he made today would affect the rest of his life.

Natalie checked her watch for the tenth time in as many minutes. It was almost eleven a.m. and Rafferty still hadn't appeared. He'd never been this late arriving before, so she could only assume that he wasn't coming in that day. Had he decided not to bother because it wasn't worth it now that she'd told him they might be better off splitting up?

The thought sent a chill of fear coursing through her and she hurried to her desk to phone him. Even though it had been her decision to tell him that, she hated to think that he'd taken her at her word. If he *really* believed that she should return to nursing, he should be prepared to fight for his beliefs!

She punched in his home phone number but there was no answer at the flat even though she let the phone ring at least a dozen times. Cutting the connection, she started to dial his cellphone number then glanced round in surprise when the office door opened and he suddenly appeared. Slamming the receiver back onto its rest, she shot to her feet and glared at him, her temper sparked by the fear that had settled into the pit of her stomach. She really didn't know what she was going to do if Rafferty went out of her life for good.

'What time do you call this?'

'I'm sorry. I should have let you know I was going to be late but something cropped up.'

Despite the apology, his tone held little sign of repentance and she glared all the harder at him. 'It really isn't good enough. When you accepted my challenge, Rafferty, you agreed to abide by my rules. I expect you to be here on time, not wander into the office whenever you feel like it.'

'I'm sorry,' he repeated flatly. 'If you want me to write out a hundred times that I must not be late in future, I'll be happy to do so.'

'Don't be ridiculous!' she snapped, swinging round so he couldn't see the angry colour that had swept up her cheeks. Rafferty was right to mock her. She was behaving more like an irate schoolteacher than the head of a blue-chip company and she needed to get a grip. It was just the thought of losing him that was making it so hard to behave sensibly.

'Shall we start this conversation again from the beginning?'

There was a weariness in his voice now that made her skin prickle and she looked at him in alarm. His face was tired and drawn, the dark circles under his eyes more pronounced than ever that day. With his black hair and aquiline features, he looked tough and unyielding as he stood in front of her desk and she felt a frisson run along her nerves. It was obvious that there was something else troubling him apart from her waspishness.

All of a sudden the fight seemed to drain out of her and she sighed. 'I'm sorry, too. I didn't mean to snap at you like that. I'm just a bit edgy…'

She broke off, not wanting to have to explain why she was so on edge. Admitting that it was the thought of them splitting up wouldn't help her reach the right decision. She had to do what was best for both of them and not allow herself to get carried away on a tide of emotion, as usually happened when they were together.

'It doesn't matter. I can't say that I'm my usual unruffled self at the moment either.' He went over to the window and stared out at the river for a moment before he turned to face her again. 'Shiloh phoned me earlier today. He wants me to head up a team he's sending over to Honduras so I'll be flying out tonight at eight o'clock.'

'I see.'

Natalie felt as though all the breath had been knocked out of her body. She knew in her heart that if Rafferty left that night, it would mean the end of their relationship. Even though she'd suggested it to him herself, it was only then that it struck her what exactly it would mean.

'You're going there because of that hurricane, I take it?' she said quietly, trying not to let him see how terrified she was. Losing Rafferty would be like losing a part of herself and the enormity of what she could be facing was almost too much to take in.

'Yes. They're already counting the casualties in thousands and they're expecting to find a lot more once the winds have died down. The whole of the coastal region is flooded and they've not managed to get anyone out there yet to see what the damage is like.' He shrugged. 'We'll be setting up camp a few miles inland so we'll be in the thick of things.'

'Did Shiloh say who else is on the team?' she asked, since it was easier to concentrate on the present than think about the future. She had no idea how she was going to live without him, but that's what she would have to do if they split up for good.

'He'd only just started ringing round when I spoke to him,' Rafferty explained, moving away from the window and sitting down on a chair. 'Ben Carstairs is going, so that's one anaesthetist. And Patsy Rush and Lauren Pierce have offered their services as well, so that's a couple of nurses. As for the rest…' He shrugged. 'Your guess is as good as mine, basically, but it won't be easy to get a team together from what Shiloh told me. He's just finished putting together a team to fly out to Mwuranda to take over from Adam Chandler, and there's a limit to how many people he can call on.'

'Two nurses, an anaesthetist and a surgeon isn't much of a team,' she agreed worriedly. 'If conditions in Honduras are as bad as has been reported on the news, you're going to need all the help you can get.'

'I know. I was wondering about asking Piers if he wanted to go along,' Rafferty said, glancing at her. 'He's quick and willing to learn so he's just the kind of person we need, but I wouldn't like to cause problems at the clinic by poaching one of their staff.'

'It will be a lot easier to find someone to cover at the clinic,' she pointed out. 'Maybe one of Piers's friends would be willing to do a stint there if it was only on a short-term basis.'

'They might. So you wouldn't object if I asked him?'

'Of course not. Why should I?'

'Because I don't want you to think that I'm encroaching on your territory, Natalie. You made it pretty plain yesterday that you weren't exactly thrilled about me volunteering to work at the clinic,' he added wryly.

'I already explained that I didn't have a problem with you working there,' she denied.

'You did, but I'm not blind. I saw the way you reacted yesterday when you saw me. You really didn't want me there, did you?'

'No.' She bit her lip but there was no point in lying. 'The clinic has been a sort of haven for me since I came back to London. Everything has been so up in the air since my father had his heart attack that it was good to be able to do something *normal* for a change.'

'It must have been hard for you these past few months,'

he said softly, and she shivered when she heard the concern in his voice.

'It wasn't easy. There was all the worry about whether Dad would pull through to begin with. Then, on top of that, there was the fact that it was vital that someone take charge of the firm in his absence. And then there was you and how you felt about me coming back to London.'

He stood up and his face was very grave as he came over to her. 'I never meant to make life difficult for you, Natalie. It's the last thing I wanted to do, believe me.'

He took hold of her hands and she held her breath, desperately hoping that he would tell her how he really felt. If he would just open up his heart and tell her that he truly loved her, she was sure they could find a way through their problems…

The sudden shrilling of his cellphone broke the spell and her shoulders slumped in defeat as he let her go to answer it. She went and sat down at her desk, wondering if she should just come straight out and ask him how he felt about her. But what on earth could she say? *Do you love me, Rafferty? Really love me with the whole of your heart and every fibre of your being?*

The trouble was that he'd always kept his emotions under wraps and she wasn't sure if he'd tell her even if she did drum up the courage to ask him. Anyway, would a declaration made under duress be worth anything? For it to really mean something, Rafferty had to tell her of his own volition that he loved her and it seemed that he wasn't prepared to do that.

'That was Ruth Thompson, the social worker from the hospital. She wants to have a word with me about Danny Kennedy. It turns out that he's only fourteen, so legally his mother must be informed as to his whereabouts.'

'Oh, no! If his mother's new partner finds out where Danny is, I don't know what will happen!' she exclaimed, setting aside her own problems for the moment. 'Danny is terrified of him.'

'That's what I need to explain to Ruth. Maybe there's a way around it if we could get in touch with Danny's father instead.'

'It would be great if you could! Maybe Danny can tell you where he works and you can contact him there,' she suggested eagerly, wishing that she'd thought of doing that herself.

'Good idea. I'll see what Ruth thinks.' Rafferty glanced at his watch and sighed. 'Look, I hate to do this but I really do have to go. I need to get this sorted out, then I have to pack. Our flight doesn't leave until eight p.m. but there's a three-hour check-in beforehand.'

'I understand.'

Natalie tried to hide her panic but it wasn't easy to remain calm when she had a horrible feeling that once Rafferty left her office it would be the end for them. Maybe it would be the best solution but she wanted them to make that decision themselves and not have it forced upon them by an airline's schedule.

'Do you?' Rafferty's voice was tinged with something that merely intensified her fears. 'I don't want you to get the wrong idea about why I'm leaving, Natalie.'

'I haven't. I won't,' she mumbled, stumbling over the words in her haste. 'You have things to do so don't worry about it. I understand. Really I do.'

She stood up abruptly, wondering if she was mad even to contemplate what she was thinking of doing. There were a dozen reasons why she shouldn't do it and only one reason why she should. However, that single reason far outweighed everything else. 'I'd better get a move on myself if I'm to have any hope of getting everything organised in time.'

'In time for what?' he asked in surprise as she hurried around the desk.

'To catch that plane with you tonight, of course.'

She took her coat off the peg, seeing the shock etched on his face. It was obvious that he hadn't expected her to do this and just for a moment she found herself wavering. However, in her heart she knew that if she let him go, he might not come back and she wasn't prepared to take that risk.

She fixed a smile to her mouth, hoping he couldn't tell how scared she was because there was no guarantee that this would achieve anything. 'You set me a challenge, don't forget. You told me to *prove* that the work I've been doing in London is as important as the work I did with Worlds Together by coming on your next mission, so that's what I'm going to do. Tell Shiloh that I shall be heading up the nursing team, will you?'

Picking up her bag, she swept out of the room. Janet was at her desk so Natalie quickly explained what was happening. Janet was obviously surprised by the speed of her decision but she quickly rallied and promised to keep things ticking over in the office while Natalie was away.

Once that was settled, Natalie realised that she needed to speak to a couple of key people whom she would have to ask to oversee the running of the company in her absence. She asked Janet to arrange a meeting in the boardroom at two o'clock that afternoon then took the lift to the ground floor. She had no idea what Rafferty had been doing while she'd been sorting out the arrangements, because he still hadn't left her office. Maybe he was too shocked to leave or worried about what she might expect from him during the forthcoming trip.

She took a deep breath as she left the building because she had no idea what she expected either. All she knew was that if she let him leave without her that night, she might never see him again and that was more than she could bear. Maybe in time she would be able to accept it but not right now. Right now she needed to be with him.

Rafferty paced the concourse as he scanned the crowd that was milling around. It was just gone four and Heathrow Airport was filling up with travellers and commuters preparing to take evening flights. The rest of the Worlds Together team were sitting outside one of the fast-food outlets having a cup of coffee while they waited for the last members of the team to arrive, but he hadn't been able to settle. How could he sit there, drinking coffee, when he had no idea if Natalie had meant what she'd said about coming with them?

He suddenly spotted her pushing her way through the crowd and his ears began to drum as blood rushed to his head. She really was coming along on the trip, and the thought made him want to turn cartwheels for joy, only the sensible side of him refused to get too excited about it. Natalie was only coming to prove a point, he reminded himself sternly. And he mustn't read too much into her decision.

'Sorry I'm late, but the traffic was horrendous. Jenkins had the devil of a job getting me here.'

'Jenkins?' Rafferty repeated, busily drinking in every detail of what she was wearing. Olive-green cargo pants and a matching T-shirt wasn't the sexiest outfit in the world and couldn't hold a candle to that evening gown she'd worn the other night. However, it was definitely good enough to stir up *his* juices!

'My father's chauffeur.'

Rafferty struggled to contain his reaction to that announcement, but it wasn't easy to have her wealth thrust into his face like that. His tone was far more acerbic than he'd intended it to be. 'It must be nice to be able to call on the services of a chauffeur and not have to suffer the usual hassles most folk go through, getting to the airport.'

'It is.'

Her smile had faded abruptly and he cursed himself when he saw her face close up. He knew he should apologise for the jibe but before he could try to make amends he heard someone shouting his name. He looked round and spotted Shiloh Smith hurrying across the concourse.

'I'm glad I managed to catch up with you before you went through passport control,' Shiloh exclaimed, shaking hands with him and kissing Natalie on the cheek.

'We'll be going through as soon as Brian and Dominic get here,' Rafferty explained shortly. He nodded towards the café. 'We were just having a last cup of coffee while we waited for them.'

'Brian's just checking in but Dominic won't be coming. That's why I needed to catch you before you left.' Shiloh's tone was unusually grim. 'I had a phone call at lunchtime to say that Dominic had been involved in an RTA on his way home from work. He's not too badly injured, thankfully enough, but he has a broken leg so he won't be going anywhere for some time.'

Rafferty groaned. 'That means we'll be a surgeon down! It's going to be really tough if there's just Larry and me. We need three surgeons minimum if we're to have any chance of keeping on top of all the work.'

'Which is why I've spent the best part of the afternoon phoning around to find a replacement.'

'And have you?' Rafferty demanded, his brows shooting up in surprise when Shiloh nodded. 'Really?'

'Yes, *really*.' Shiloh laughed. 'It's little short of a miracle, isn't it? But we came up trumps. You probably know her, in fact—Joanna Archer, Head of Surgery at St Leonard's.'

'Of course I know Joanna!' Rafferty exclaimed. 'She's a first-rate surgeon although I didn't know she was one of our volunteers.'

'Officially, she isn't, but her husband has worked for us a couple of times. You might know him as well—Dylan

Archer?' Shiloh carried on when he nodded. 'I phoned Dylan to see if he could give us a hand as soon as I heard about Dominic, but he can't get away at the moment. He's just taken up a new consultancy post and he needs to oversee the arrangements for his new team. Anyway, Joanna must have overheard what he was saying because she offered her services instead.' Shiloh broke off and grinned. 'Here she is now, in fact.'

Rafferty turned round and smiled when he saw Joanna approaching them. It had been a couple of years since he'd seen her and he couldn't help thinking how well she looked as they shook hands. Her husband and son had come to see her off and he felt a lump suddenly come to his throat when he saw the little boy, which was odd because he'd never thought much about having children. His life had seemed complete up to now and children hadn't been an issue, but as he looked at the boy he was overwhelmed by a sudden sense of longing for a child of his own.

He glanced at Natalie as she bent to speak to the boy and felt his heart catch when it struck him that the only woman he wanted to have a child with was her. She would be a wonderful mother, too, and would give their child all the love he or she could ever need, but how would she feel about the idea of them having children?

It was as though all the fears and uncertainties he'd harboured had suddenly crystallised into this one point: could Natalie see him as the future father of her children, or would she want a man who was more her social equal?

CHAPTER EIGHT

'GET another litre of saline into her, stat. She's so dehydrated that her whole system is in danger of shutting down.'

Rafferty tossed his soiled gloves into the waste sack and picked up a fresh pair. It had been like a conveyor belt all morning as one casualty after another had been brought in. Most of them were children because it was always the youngest and the weakest who came off worst in any disaster. Many had been crushed when buildings had fallen on them, others had been swept away by the floods which had swamped the coastal region of the country and the rest had been victims of the mayhem which had broken out after the hurricane had hit. It was hard not to feel overwhelmed by the sheer scale of the disaster, but it wouldn't help if he gave in to his emotions so he hid them behind a veneer of calm.

'What have we got here?' he rapped out, stopping beside the next in the long line of beds that had been placed in the triage area of the camp.

The ground crew had worked miracles to get everything set up so quickly. As well as the all-important theatre tent, there was a separate tent for triage and treatment of a non-surgical nature, two tents to be used as wards, plus their own living quarters. It was barely ten hours since they'd landed at Comayagua Palmerola airport and in that time they'd got themselves up and running, if not at full speed then at something rapidly approaching it. Rafferty knew that the success of the operation so far was partly Natalie's doing because she'd pulled out all the stops to get everything ready. It just seemed to prove his point that she was wasted at Palmer's—not that it was his main concern any longer, of course.

'Five-year-old with extensive crush injuries.'

Natalie was all business as she talked him through the status of his next patient and he made himself emulate her attitude because it would achieve nothing to give in to this feeling of panic that was humming away inside him. He had no idea if Natalie thought he would be a good father for her children, but he would have to find out the answer at some point because it was important that he know the truth.

'Where did they find him?' he demanded, focusing on the child because he couldn't deal with thoughts like that right now.

'He was buried in the ruins of the school. Most of the people from his village had gone there to shelter so there are dozens of casualties still being dug out.'

'Do we know how long he was trapped?' Rafferty asked, bending over so he could examine the boy.

Both his legs were badly bruised and swollen although Rafferty couldn't detect any fractures. The upper part of his body was unmarked and he was breathing unaided, but Rafferty was too experienced to take that as a sign the boy would recover. Crush syndrome—whereby large amounts of protein pigments found their way into the bloodstream from the damaged muscles—could impair his kidney function. If the toxins that would normally be excreted by the kidneys built up, it would cause kidney failure. He knew that the boy would need dialysis to prevent that happening and that the machine they had brought with them was currently being used by another patient.

'No. Most of the people they've dug out so far are too badly injured to question,' Natalie explained.

'So he could have been there at least a day and probably longer.' Rafferty shook his head. 'There's no way he'll escape with his kidney function unimpaired. We need to get him onto dialysis as soon as possible.'

'The machine's in use.' Natalie glanced round and beckoned Piers over. 'Can you check how the patient on dialysis is doing? We need to know realistically what his chances are.'

Piers glanced uncertainly at the child. 'You mean you might have to take him off the machine so this boy can use it?'

Rafferty nodded, knowing how hard it would be for the younger doctor to accept such a decision. 'If the patient who's currently undergoing haemodialysis isn't going to recover then the boy should be given a chance. It's a tough call but it's essential we make this kind of decision when facilities have to be rationed.'

'I understand.' Piers didn't say anything else as he hurried away. However, Rafferty could tell that he was upset about having to make a life-or-death judgement.

'He'll cope,' Natalie said softly, and he looked at her in surprise because he hadn't realised his expression had been so revealing.

'You think so?'

'Yes. Piers is a good doctor and a very caring person but he's a realist, too. He'll find it hard but he'll accept the need to make a difficult decision in a situation like this.'

'I hope so,' Rafferty said bluntly. 'If he doesn't then he's going to find this job really hard going.'

'Just give him time to settle in and he'll be fine.'

She gave him a quick smile and he looked away when he felt heat buzz along his veins. He couldn't afford to let his concentration waver. He carried on with his examination and had logged up a fractured left wrist by the time Piers came back to update them on the status of the patient currently undergoing haemodialysis.

'I've just spoken to Joanna and she said to tell you that he's holding his own. Apparently, the dialysis has made a huge difference and she's confident that he's going to make it if we can keep him on the machine.'

'Fine,' Rafferty agreed. He certainly wasn't going to question Joanna's judgement. 'We'll have to try a different approach for our young friend, then. I take it that you know how peritoneal dialysis works?'

'Yes, but only from what I've read in a textbook. I've never seen it actually done,' Piers admitted with a trace of excitement in his voice.

Rafferty smiled to himself because it was good to know that Natalie's faith in the younger man hadn't been misplaced. She'd always been a good judge of character, he thought, then wasn't sure why the idea should seem so important all of a sudden.

'Peritoneal dialysis makes use of the body's own filtering membrane, i.e. the peritoneum,' he explained briskly, confining himself to work rather than allowing his thoughts to start wandering off at a tangent again. He picked up a pen and quickly drew a diagram on the back of the clipboard.

'A small incision is made just here in the abdomen and a catheter inserted into the peritoneal cavity. Dialysate is passed through the catheter and left for several hours while waste products and excess water from the blood vessels lining the peritoneal cavity seep through the peritoneal membrane. The resulting fluid is drained off through the catheter into the empty bag.'

'And that's what you're thinking of doing in this instance?' Piers questioned eagerly.

'Yes. I'd prefer him to have haemodialysis but it just isn't possible so this is the next best thing. Get scrubbed up and you can see how it's done.'

Rafferty turned to Natalie as a delighted Piers hurried away. 'I'm going to take the boy straight to Theatre. We daren't wait or we'll lose him. Will you assist me?'

'Of course.'

Natalie didn't waste time as she called Lauren over and explained what was happening. Within a very short space of time they were in Theatre. Rafferty glanced at Ben, who was acting as his anaesthetist, and as soon as he got the go-ahead he set to work, feeling a deep sense of satisfaction at how smoothly the procedure progressed. Natalie seemed able to anticipate his every need so that he didn't have to ask for whatever he needed. They'd always worked well together in Theatre, though, their actions so in tune that it was like a well-honed routine.

He sighed to himself as he finished securing the catheter. If only their life outside Theatre were as harmonious, they wouldn't be having all these problems. But that was like wishing for the moon to drop into his lap and it wasn't going to happen. He and Natalie either had to find some way to work through their problems or call it a day.

Natalie handed Rafferty a piece of tape and waited while he secured the catheter into place. Every time they were in Theatre together, she was struck afresh by his skill. She'd worked with a lot of surgeons over the years but few had possessed his delicacy of touch. He was swift but sure, never cutting needlessly and always mindful of the extent of the scarring that would be left behind. It was little wonder that his patients praised him so highly after they recovered. A patient under Rafferty's care was very fortunate indeed, and her heart swelled with pride at the thought.

'That's about all I can do for now.' He suddenly looked up and she hastily gathered her thoughts.

'At least he has a fighting chance now,' she said evenly, placing the last of the instruments they'd used onto the trolley.

'Let's hope so.'

There was a faintly depressed note in his deep voice and she glanced uncertainly at him because it wasn't like him to exhibit any doubts about his work. 'Are you worried about him?' she asked, choosing her words with care because she sensed that his concern wasn't wholly for their patient.

Was he worrying about them? she wondered all of a sudden, and just as suddenly knew it was true. It troubled her to think that their relationship was intruding on his work when he'd always been so focused before. It made her see that they had to resolve the situation soon because it wasn't fair to either of them to carry on this way. However, it was the thought of what the resolution might be that was so difficult to deal with.

'I'd worry about anyone in his condition,' he replied tersely, turning away from the operating table.

Natalie didn't say anything else. She'd had her answer and it was her own fault for asking if it hadn't been to her liking. She cleared everything away, carefully checking the instruments against her list to make sure they were all accounted for before she took them through to be cleaned and sterilised.

By the time that was done, Joanna had arrived with another patient so Natalie ended up staying on to assist her. It was gone seven before they finally left Theatre and everyone was in the mess tent having dinner. She heard Joanna groan as they crossed the compound together.

'I'm so hungry I could eat a horse!'

'I hope you mean that because I'm not sure what's on the menu tonight,' Natalie said, grinning at her. She ducked inside the tent then paused and looked around for somewhere for them to sit. All the seats seemed to be taken but Brian must have spotted them coming in because he stood up and waved.

'I've just about finished here so one of you can have my seat,' he offered when they went over to him. 'And there's a free place over there on Rafferty's table.'

Natalie glanced at Joanna. 'Which do you fancy?'

'I'm easy,' Joanna replied, stifling a yawn. 'Oh, excuse me! I'm obviously not toned up for this hectic pace yet.'

Natalie laughed as she gently pushed her down onto the chair. 'Sit yourself down before you fall down! Maybe Brian will behave like the perfect gentleman and fetch your dinner for you.'

Brian immediately offered to fetch Joanna a tray so Natalie left them to it while she went to collect her own meal. She took her tray over to Rafferty's table. Ben was sitting with him and Patsy and Piers as well, and they all looked up when she approached.

'Mind if I join you?' she asked, more as a matter of form than because she thought they would object to her sitting with them.

'Of course not.'

Rafferty shuffled along the bench to give her some room so Natalie plonked her tray on the table and sat down. Picking up her fork, she dug it into the savoury concoction of meat and vegetables which she'd been served. All the catering was done by their ground crew and the meals were usually very basic—stew and shepherd's pie, sausage and mash, that kind of thing. Piers grinned as he watched her fork up a mouthful of the stew.

'I was afraid we might end up eating bush tucker so it was a huge relief to see what was on the menu tonight.'

'Grubs and bugs, you mean?' Natalie chuckled. 'It can be arranged if you fancy it. I'm sure Wally, who's in charge of the crew, could turn out a mean scorpion pie if he set his mind to it.'

'No, thank you very much!' Piers shuddered. 'I'm more than happy to stick to what I know.'

'Can't say I blame you,' Rafferty put in. He turned to Natalie. 'Remember those meals we had when we were on Baffin Island?'

'Do I?' She groaned. 'My stomach still hasn't recovered!'

'Why? What happened?' Piers demanded. 'Baffin Island is

off the coast of Canada, isn't it, so what were you doing there?'

'That's right. It's off the northeast coast of Canada, very close to the Arctic Circle. It's mainly the Inuit who live there and although there's some mining carried out, they tend to stick to the old way of life,' Rafferty explained. 'We'd gone there because there'd been an outbreak of measles. More than thirty people had died so we offered to help run a vaccination programme.'

He paused to drink some coffee before carrying on. 'We were working closely with the Canadian authorities and they'd arranged to have our supplies airlifted to one of the more remote settlements where we were planning to set up camp. Everything was going very smoothly until one of the helicopters was blown off course and managed to drop the crates containing our food supplies into the sea.'

'And as luck would have it, there was a terrible storm brewing so they were unable to send out a replacement shipment,' Natalie put in, chuckling. 'It meant we had to eat what the local people gave us, which turned out to be a selection of raw whale and seal meat!'

'Oh, gross!' Piers turned a delicate shade of green. 'I don't know how you ate it. I couldn't have done.'

'We didn't have a choice,' Rafferty pointed out mildly. 'It was either eat it or starve, although I have to say that I wouldn't be in a hurry to repeat the experience.'

'Me neither,' Natalie agreed, smiling at him.

Their eyes met and she felt her heart leap when she saw the warmth in his gaze. It was a moment of closeness that had been all too rare recently and she only wished that it would last. Deep down she knew that they could reach a true understanding if they could shut out everything else, but it wasn't possible to divorce themselves from life. If their relationship was to last, they had to learn how to overcome their problems, not avoid them. It shouldn't have been that difficult really. If they loved one another, they could find a way round all the uncertainties, but did Rafferty love her enough to try to find a solution? It always came back to that same question and she was no nearer to knowing what the answer was.

The thought put a bit of a dampener on her mood. Natalie finished her supper, only joining in the conversation when someone asked her a direct question. Rafferty was unusually quiet, too, and she couldn't help wondering if he was thinking much the same as her. It was all very unsettling, in fact, so she was glad when she could make her escape at last.

She went straight back to her tent and lay down on her bed but even though she was exhausted after the busy day they'd had, it was impossible to sleep. Joanna came back a short time later and they chatted while she was getting ready for bed but Natalie was still wide awake long after the other woman had fallen asleep.

In the end, she got up and left the tent, hoping that a breath of fresh air would help to settle her down. The camp was winding down for the night and there was just a skeleton staff left on duty to take care of their patients. Natalie carefully bypassed the areas where she might have bumped into anyone and left the camp, following the path that led to the village which was the main site of the excavation work.

They were just a few miles from the coast and the whole area had been devastated by the hurricane. The local people earned their living by growing bananas and plantains for export but most of the trees had been uprooted during the storm. Now great swathes of dried mud covered the fields and she sighed as she saw the damage that had been caused. It was going to be very hard for the people to rebuild their lives after such a disaster and it made her own problems seem very insignificant by comparison. Surely two intelligent people should be able to sort out their differences?

She rounded a bend and ground to a halt when she spotted

a figure up ahead. There was no moon that night so it was very dark along this section of the path. She could just make out the outlines of the search-and-rescue teams' tents in the distance, but the camp was still some way off. She was very conscious all of a sudden that she was on her own and was just about to go back rather than risk a confrontation with a stranger when the man turned and she gasped in relief when she realised it was Rafferty.

'Oh, you gave me a shock!' she exclaimed as he came towards her. 'I didn't realise it was you at first.'

'What are you doing out here on your own?' he demanded gruffly.

'I couldn't sleep, so I decided to go for a walk in the hope it would help to settle me down,' she explained, knowing he had every right to be angry with her. It was a cardinal rule that members of the team shouldn't wander about on their own at night, and she'd just broken it.

'I thought you had more sense than to go wandering around on your own. Anything could have happened to you out here at this time of night.'

'I know, and I'm sorry. I didn't do it intentionally to upset you, although everything I do nowadays seems to annoy you. You'd probably object if you thought I was breathing at the wrong rate!' she snapped back, because she was tired of being made to feel that nothing she did met with his approval.

'Don't be so ridiculous!' His expression had turned thunderous. 'You're behaving like a child now because you don't like to admit that you were wrong to wander about.'

'So I'm childish now, am I? Anything else? I mean, you may as well get it all off your chest while you have the chance.' She put her hands on her hips and glared at him. 'You've been waiting to have a go at me, Rafferty, so don't hold back.'

'I have not been waiting to have a go at you, as you put it,' he retorted, brushing past her. 'Now, it's late and I think we'd be better off in bed instead of standing here squabbling.'

'I am *not* squabbling!' She grabbed hold of his arm and stopped him, too incensed by his high-handedness to care about what she was doing.

'No? Well, forgive me if I don't agree. In fact, I'd say it's all we ever do. We argue and squabble and I, for one, am sick and tired of it.'

His green eyes blazed into hers and her breath caught when she saw the emotion they held because his response seemed way over the top for the seriousness of her crime. She had no idea why he was so angry with her but instinct told her that she needed to defuse the situation before it got completely out of control.

'Look, Rafferty—' she began, but he didn't give her a chance to finish.

He shook off her hand and her heart sank when she saw the set expression on his face. 'Don't bother, Natalie. There isn't any point trying to smooth things over again. Every time we talk to each other we end up arguing, and we can't carry on like this. It isn't fair to either of us. We have to accept that the situation isn't going to change and get on with our lives.'

'What do you mean by that?' she whispered, her throat constricting with fear so that her voice sounded thin and shaky when it emerged.

'That our relationship isn't working and never will work. We come from two different worlds and that's why we never agree about anything, that's why we're continually arguing.'

'How can you say that? You make it sound as though we have nothing in common and it isn't true. We do the same type of job and we both care passionately about the same issues—'

'And we're both too stubborn to accept that sometimes you can't *make* a relationship work. That's what we've been doing, isn't it? We've been trying to make it work—like fitting a round peg into a square hole, pushing and shoving to make everything fit together—but it's never going to happen. No matter how hard we try, our relationship still isn't going to fulfil our expectations, is it?'

He took hold of her by the shoulders and drew her to him, held her for a single heartbeat then let her go, and Natalie knew without the shadow of a doubt that this was the end, that it was the last time he would ever hold her in his arms.

She reached out to him in panic, gripping hold of his hands, her fingers digging into his flesh because she refused to accept that they couldn't work things out if they tried. 'You're wrong! We can make it work, Rafferty, if we love each other enough. That's all it will take to solve our problems.'

'I wish it were that simple.'

He gently withdrew his hands and she felt her heart stutter to a halt when she saw the shuttered expression on his face. It was obvious then that he didn't agree. Maybe he knew in his own heart that he could never love her the way she wanted him to, love her to the exclusion of everything else, and there was no way she could make him.

Tears welled into her eyes and she spun round because she refused to let him see her crying. If he hadn't been moved by her pleas then she didn't want him to be moved by her tears. The last thing she wanted from him was pity!

She ran back along the path, ignoring his pleas for her to stop, because there was no point in talking any more. Maybe she hadn't asked him how he felt about her, but she hadn't needed to because she had her answer now. He didn't love her as much as she loved him and there was nothing else to say. All she could do was to try and get through the next few days with her dignity intact, even if her heart was in tatters, and then they could go their separate ways.

Joanna was fast asleep when she went back to their tent

so Natalie lay down on her bunk and buried her face in her pillow so that her sobs wouldn't wake her, yet oddly after a few minutes she found that she couldn't cry any more. It was as though all her emotions had suddenly frozen solid and she couldn't feel anything except a kind of numbness and disbelief that it had actually happened. It was a relief because all the feelings that were churning around inside her were too awful to deal with.

Natalie closed her eyes and tried to sleep because she knew that in the morning it would be different. When she saw Rafferty again, that was when it would hit her afresh, but she would have to get used to the idea of being without him because she wasn't going to try and change his mind. There was no point. He didn't love her the way she loved him and she refused to settle for scraps. This really was the end of their affair.

CHAPTER NINE

'GET that shifted immediately. I don't expect to see sacks of clinical waste lying around. If you can't maintain an acceptable level of hygiene, you may as well go home.'

Rafferty strode out of the ward before he really let rip. He knew he'd been a bit hard on Patsy but if there was one thing he wouldn't tolerate, it was the lowering of standards. Cross-infection was a major hazard even in the best-equipped hospitals and it was doubly dangerous in a situation like this.

'How dare you speak to one of my nurses like that?'

He swung round when Natalie followed him out of the tent, feeling his stomach lurch when he saw the fury on her face. It had been two days since they'd had that talk, two days during which time he'd hardly been able to think straight because of what he'd done. He had ended their relationship, told her that he no longer wanted her in his life, and it felt as though he had ripped out his own heart and ground it into the dust.

'I shall address the staff any way I see fit,' he snapped back, pain bolstering up his anger. 'Although if you'd been doing your job properly in the first place, I wouldn't have needed to speak to Patsy like that. There is no excuse for leaving clinical waste lying about the ward, as you very well know.'

'For your information, that sack had been put there exactly five minutes before you arrived and the reason it was left there was because one of the patients suffered a cardiac arrest. Patsy and I had to drop everything while we resuscitated him.'

She strode towards him, her beautiful face set, her eyes

haunted, and it was the latter that hurt more than the angry words could ever have done. To see the evidence of the damage he had caused was more than he could bear, but he knew that he mustn't weaken otherwise he could end up making the situation worse.

'The patient was stable when I arrived, which means that you'd had ample time to clear everything away.' He held up his hand when she started to protest. 'Don't bother, Natalie. I'm not interested in your excuses. If you aren't up to the job then you should go back to London as well. You wouldn't have to worry about the problems of cross-infection once you were safely back in your office.'

He spun round, not giving her a chance to reply. He knew he'd overstepped the mark by saying that, but it was done now and that was the end of it, just as it was the end of all the hopes he'd harboured once for their future together. It wouldn't be *him* spending his life with Natalie now but some other guy far more suited to the role of her husband and the father of her kids.

It would be a picture-perfect life, too, he thought grimly. Just like those advertisements they showed on television—a beautiful mother, a handsome father and a clutch of happy kids. Throw in a cute little puppy and the result would be the ideal nuclear family. Oh, hell!

Rafferty cursed roundly as he let himself into the theatre tent. There was a list of patients a yard long scheduled for surgery that day and he desperately needed to get his brain into gear. The number of casualties had been boosted that morning when several dozen people had been recovered from the sacristy of the local church. Despite all the odds stacked against them, they had survived thus far and he didn't intend to let them down by not being properly focused.

'Oh, hi! I was wondering where you'd got to. I'm taking a break now so Theatre's all yours.'

Rafferty summoned a smile as Joanna came into the changing area because he didn't want everyone knowing what had gone on. So far they seemed to have avoided any gossip—at least, nobody had said anything to him about him and Natalie splitting up. He could only assume that she was as keen as he was to keep their private life private and hadn't told anyone the news. Or maybe the truth was that she hadn't thought it worth mentioning they'd split up for good. After all, their relationship had been on the rocks for ages so nobody would be shocked to hear that they had called it a day.

The thought stung and he had to make a conscious effort to put it out of his mind. 'How's it gone so far?'

'Not too bad, considering.' Joanna stripped off her gown and dropped it into the hamper. 'I was expecting a lot more problems because I'd assumed that everyone would be very dehydrated. It's four days since the church collapsed and that's a long time for people to go without water. However, it turned out that they'd been drinking the Communion wine that had been stored in the sacristy. Fortunately, the local priest waters it down so there was very little alcohol in it and it kept everyone going until the rescue team found them.'

'It appears miracles can and do happen,' Rafferty observed wryly.

Joanna laughed. 'So it seems. Anyway, I've got down to here on the list…' she handed him the clipboard and pointed to a spot midway down the long list of names '…so the rest are all yours. Is Natalie going to assist you?'

'It's Patsy's turn in Theatre today,' he replied flatly, because he didn't want to think about Natalie and what had just happened…

He sighed as Joanna bade him goodbye and left. There was no way that he could stop thinking about Natalie. Her name was constantly on his mind, like a tune that kept playing over and over inside his head. He longed to tell her that he'd made a mistake and that he didn't want them to split up, but how could he do that when it would start the whole process all over again? He had to accept that they weren't right for each other and that she would be better off without him. OK, so it hurt like hell to admit it, but what choice did he have? Did he really want to go on making her life miserable?

The answer to that question was all too clear. Rafferty knew that he wouldn't be able to live with himself if he went on upsetting her the way he had been doing. Stripping off his T-shirt, he grabbed a towel and headed for the shower. He was just drying himself off when he heard someone coming into the tent. He poked his head round the curtain, expecting it to be Patsy. He knew that he'd been much too hard on her and he wanted to apologise before they went into Theatre. However, it wasn't Patsy standing by the bench, getting undressed, but Natalie herself.

'What are you doing here?' he barked, ill-temper providing the easiest outlet for all the emotions that were rioting around inside him. On the one hand he was determined to behave sensibly, but on the other hand the sight of her standing there in a skimpy little T-shirt and a pair of cotton panties had driven any sensible thoughts from his head. All he could do was react, and he did.

'Scrubbing up to assist you,' she replied shortly, stripping off her T-shirt and tossing it onto the pile of clothes.

Rafferty swallowed a groan because the sight of her beautiful body in the serviceable cotton underwear was more than enough to make him want to reconsider his decision. It took a massive effort of will not to haul her into the shower with him as she stalked past the stall to take a towel off the shelf.

'I thought Patsy was rostered for Theatre this afternoon,' he bit out, desperately trying to remember all the reasons why he mustn't weaken.

'She was. However, I decided she'd had enough of you for one day so I offered to trade places with her. Funnily enough, she didn't object.'

Natalie wrapped the towel around herself and Rafferty sighed in dismay as he was suddenly deprived of the sight of her delectable body. It struck him all of a sudden just how long it had been since he'd held her naked in his arms, and just how much he wanted to do so again. The thought was enough to send his temper spiralling. He was supposed to be acting sensibly, not tormenting himself!

'If Patsy has a complaint about my behaviour, she is perfectly entitled to raise it with me.'

'And risk another bawling-out?' Natalie's delicate brows arched derisively. 'I don't think so. It's bad enough that you saw fit to take her to task in the first place. Your quarrel is with me, Rafferty, not Patsy or anyone else on this team.'

'Don't flatter yourself!' The rebuke had touched an already raw nerve and he glared at her. 'What I said to Patsy had nothing whatsoever to do with what went on between us.'

'No? Obviously, I'm mistaken, then. I apologise.'

She didn't say anything else as she went into the neighbouring stall and swished the curtain across. Rafferty ground his teeth because he hated admitting that she was right. If he hadn't been so screwed up about them splitting up, he would have handled things very differently that day, and it didn't make him feel good to know that he'd treated one of the team so unfairly.

He grabbed a clean scrub suit off the pile and dragged it on then went through to the scrub area and finished getting ready, lathering his hands and forearms with antiseptic solution and scrubbing under his nails with even more vigour than usual. Natalie arrived just as he was finishing off, looking professional to a fault with her hair neatly tucked under a disposable cap. She took a fresh gown off the pile and held it out for him to slide his arms into the sleeves then stepped around him and fastened the ties up the back.

'Thank you,' Rafferty said curtly, waiting while she took a pair of extra-large gloves out of the box. She held them out so he could slip his hands into them then reached for a second pair and repeated the procedure before he was ready to go through to Theatre where Jack Huxley was waiting with his first patient already anaesthetised.

'Everything OK?' Rafferty asked, more as a matter of form because Jack would soon have told him if it wasn't.

'Ready when you are,' Jack replied cheerfully, nodding to Natalie who had joined them.

Rafferty quickly read through the patient's notes to remind himself about her injuries before he set to work. Dilia Meléndez was one of the people who'd been found in the sacristy. She had a fractured pelvis so his first job was to check if there was any soft-tissue damage. He set to work, grimacing when he quickly discovered a large tear in her bladder.

'I'll need to flush out the abdominal and pelvic cavities,' he said, glancing at Natalie, who had taken up her usual position beside him.

'I've got everything ready,' she assured him, turning to fetch one of the bags of saline from the trolley.

Rafferty quickly flushed away the urine that had leaked from the young woman's ruptured bladder, taking extra care in the hope that it might help to stave off any infection. He knew it was something of a vain hope because Dilia had been trapped in the ruins for several days and infection was almost certain to have set in by now. Once he was sure that he'd done all he could to clean the area, he stitched the tear in her bladder, repaired her pelvis and closed up, suturing the layers of muscle and skin with his usual care and attention to detail.

'She'll need broad-spectrum antibiotics,' he told Natalie, who now held the clipboard containing Dilia's notes. 'Can you make a note on her chart to say that I want to know if there's any sign of infection starting up? I may need to open her up and flush everything out again.'

'Got that.'

She made a note on the chart then wheeled Dilia out of Theatre. Lauren was in charge of Recovery that day and he could hear Natalie passing along his instructions. He sighed as he stripped off his gloves and went to scrub up again. He'd had no right to criticise her before. There was no one better at the job than Natalie and he would have to apologise for what he'd said to her, although he would need to be careful that he kept strictly to what he'd said about her work, of course. He didn't dare apologise for upsetting her the other night, couldn't take the risk of letting her think that he'd had a change of heart. He had made the right decision and had made it for the right reasons, too, no matter what she believed.

He turned off the water and his heart felt like lead because he knew there was no going back now. Once they left Honduras, he and Natalie would part for good.

Natalie was exhausted by the time she left Theatre several hours later. It had been a long and busy day but she knew that it wasn't just the pressure of work that was making her feel so worn out. She'd barely slept since the other night and her body had reached exhaustion point. She kept going over and over what Rafferty had said to her, wondering if he'd meant it even though she knew in her heart that he had. He didn't want her any more, and the thought was like red-hot pain constantly stabbing through her heart.

'You're looking very glum. What's up?'

She glanced round when Joanna caught up with her and dredged up a weary smile. 'Oh, I'm just tired, I expect.'

'And that's all it is?' Joanna sighed when Natalie looked uncertainly at her. 'Look, I'm not trying to pry but I heard you crying the other night when we were in bed.'

'I'm sorry. I didn't mean to wake you.'

'Don't be silly. That wasn't what I meant.'

Joanne touched her lightly on the shoulder, her face full

of sympathy, and for some reason it just seemed to get past all Natalie's defences. She'd tried so hard not to let the situation get her down but it was so awful that she didn't know which way to turn. Rafferty didn't want her any more and it felt as though her whole world had caved in on itself, so it was no wonder that tears immediately sprang to her eyes.

'What you need is a nice hot cup of tea,' Joanna said firmly, steering her towards the mess tent. She found them a table in the corner and sat Natalie down while she went to fetch their drinks.

Natalie blew her nose and dried her eyes, smiling gratefully when Joanna came back a few minutes later with two mugs of dark brown tea.

'Thanks. I need this.'

'There's nothing like a cuppa to help put the world to rights,' Joanna observed bracingly, sitting down.

'The age-old panacea for all ills,' she agreed, wishing it would work its magic in this instance.

'Oh, that it were,' Joanna observed drolly. She took a sip of the tannin-laden liquid and shuddered. 'Oh, boy. That should put hair on our chests!'

Natalie chuckled despite her downbeat mood. 'I'm sure your husband will appreciate that when you get back home.'

'Knowing Dylan, he'd probably take it in his stride. The most wonderful thing about being married is that you no longer have to put up a front. You learn to love each other's faults as well as their good points because it's what makes them the person they are.'

'You're lucky to have found someone who loves you like that,' she said wistfully.

'I am. Very lucky indeed, and I know it, too.' Joanna smiled at her. 'It's what marriage is all about, isn't it? A willingness to compromise and accept one another, warts and all. I used to think that life couldn't get any better than it was when I first met Dylan. There was an instant attraction between us, you see, a real spark that was both scary and exhilarating, so it was a marvellous time. But being married is even better. Knowing that you can rely totally on someone and that he'll always be there for you, no matter what, gives you a kind of inner peace.'

'I envy you,' Natalie said honestly. 'To find that kind of closeness is something really special. I thought that I...'

She broke off because she wasn't sure if she should tell Joanna about the hopes she'd had once for Rafferty and herself.

'You thought you'd found that same sort of closeness with Rafferty,' Joanna finished for her, smiling when Natalie looked at her in surprise. 'Please, don't be embarrassed. It's obvious that you two have something special between you.'

'We do...or, rather, I thought we did.' Natalie picked up her mug then put it down again when she realised that her hands were shaking.

'So what's gone wrong?' Joanna prompted gently.

'Rafferty has decided that we're not suited and that we should split up for good.' Her voice cracked and she bit her lip, not wanting to make a show of herself by breaking down in public.

'And how do you feel about it?'

'I don't know. That's the silly thing about it all. I'd got to the point of wondering if we should finish it rather than keep on making each other miserable, but now that it's happened...' She tailed off and shrugged.

'And you can't see any way around your problems?'

'Not really. Our relationship has always been volatile but I thought we'd sort things out in the end if we both wanted it enough. Now there's no point even trying, because if Rafferty had felt the same about me as I feel about him then he wouldn't have given up on us, would he?'

'Maybe he thought he was doing what was best for you,' Joanna suggested slowly.

Natalie sighed. 'I wish I could believe that. But why didn't he tell me that was the reason he was ending our relationship, if that was true?'

'Maybe he didn't want you to talk him out of it.' Joanna laughed wryly. 'Men have some very funny ideas at times. They come over all noble and decide that they have to do the honourable thing, even if it isn't really what they want to do.'

'And you think that Rafferty might have done the same—decided that he should step aside because it was the honourable thing to do?'

'I don't know. But it's a thought, isn't it, and certainly worth considering? Maybe you should ask him straight out why he decided to end your relationship at this stage.'

'And what if he tells me that he doesn't want to be with me any more?'

'Then at least you'll know for certain rather than second-guessing, won't you?' Joanna patted her hand. 'Anything has to be better than that, Natalie. Surely?'

Natalie knew that Joanna was right. She needed to know once and for all how Rafferty felt about her, because she couldn't keep on torturing herself this way. Her spirits suddenly lifted. If Joanna was also right about his reasons for ending their relationship, she would make him see that his fears were groundless. She didn't want him doing the *honourable* thing. She just wanted him to love her!

There was no opportunity to speak to Rafferty that night because the search-and-rescue teams discovered more survivors. The first of them began to arrive before they'd finished their tea, in fact, so she and Joanna went back to Theatre. Fifteen casualties in all were brought into the camp and twelve of them needed surgery so it was a case of wheeling one out and the next one in. It was three a.m. by the time they finished and they were all exhausted.

Natalie sent Patsy and Lauren off to bed because there was no point in them missing out on their sleep. She finished clearing up then took the instruments through to the sluice room to be cleaned and sterilised in readiness for the following day. Piers had been working between both theatres—helping out wherever he was needed—and he looked grey with tiredness when he came and propped his lanky frame against the sink.

'I am *shattered*! I thought the hours were long as a junior house man but this beats it hands down. How on earth do you keep up this pace?'

'It isn't always as bad as this,' Natalie assured him, closing the autoclave door. 'It was just unfortunate that they happened to find those people when they did. If only casualties could be dug out between the hours of nine and five, our lives would be a lot easier,' she added, her tongue very firmly in her cheek.

'I wish!' Piers grimaced as he pushed himself into an upright position. 'OK, so which way is the exit? If you could point me in the right direction, I'll be eternally grateful.'

'Here you go.' Natalie gave him a little shove towards the exit, grinning when he reeled across the tent. 'Night-night, sleep tight. Mind the bugs don't bite,' she called after him.

'They can bite all they like because I won't feel them,' he muttered as he staggered out through the flap.

Natalie chuckled to herself as she started to wipe down the trolley with disinfectant. Poor Piers would think twice the next time he was invited along on one of their missions!

'That's it, then. Everything present and accounted for?'

She glanced up when Rafferty appeared, feeling her heart welling with concern when she saw how exhausted he looked. If Piers had looked grey with fatigue, Rafferty's skin bore the colourless appearance of total exhaustion. No wonder, too, because he must have clocked up almost twenty hours in Theatre that day and it was far too much for anyone.

'Yes. Everything's just about sorted out now so it's time for bed, I think,' she replied lightly, because he wouldn't thank her for worrying about him. He'd always been very independent and had never relied on anyone else to help him, and it struck her all of a sudden just how strange that was. Most people relied to some extent on the people they worked with, but not Rafferty. He never asked for a favour, rarely delegated and was always the first to volunteer when it came to extra work.

Was it the result of the way he'd been brought up? she found herself wondering.

Being passed from pillar to post while he'd been growing up must have meant that he'd had no one except himself to rely on and that was why he was so self-sufficient. It could also explain why he was so wary of showing his emotions. He'd never had the opportunity to form an attachment to anyone because he'd been moved so frequently, so he'd learned to keep his feelings hidden.

It was as though she was seeing the situation through fresh eyes and it shocked her that she'd never given any thought before to the full effect his past must have had on him. She'd been too caught up by the need to convince him that her family's wealth didn't matter to take account of the reasons why it did. She'd had loving parents and stability while he'd had very little affection and lots of uncertainty—was it any wonder that he was afraid of making a mistake over her?

'I'm so tired that I don't know if I'll be able to sleep.'

Rafferty followed her out of the tent, pausing to turn off the generator so that they were plunged into darkness. There were just the security lights left on now to guide them across the compound. Everywhere was very quiet. Even the sound of digging had stopped as the search-and-rescue teams had finished working for the night. It lent an air of intimacy to their surroundings, which wasn't lost on Natalie as they made their way through the camp.

'Maybe you should go for a walk?' she suggested, her voice sounding husky as nerves suddenly set in. Was this the right moment to ask him why he'd ended their relationship? Bearing in mind these new revelations she'd had to explain his behaviour, it seemed even more important that she make him tell her the truth. It was just the fact that he was so exhausted that stopped her blurting it out.

'I don't think my legs would support me.' He groaned as they stopped outside his tent. 'I'm not even sure if I can make it as far as my bed. If I keel over, just leave me here and I'll be fine!'

Natalie drummed up a laugh but it was hard to know what to do for the best. She had a funny feeling that she would get only one shot at this and she didn't want to waste it by choosing the wrong moment.

'It would save time, I suppose,' she said lightly. 'You'd be all ready for the next round in the morning if you slept there.'

'Don't!' Rafferty rolled his eyes. 'I don't even want to *think* about going through a repeat of today.' He took a deep breath then bent down and unzipped the flap on his tent. 'Right, I'm going to bed and I'm going to sleep. It's just a question of mind over matter, isn't it? Goodnight, Natalie. I'll see you in the morning.'

'Goodnight,' she echoed as he ducked inside the tent. There was nothing else she could say now. She'd missed her opportunity so now she would have to bide her time and hope that there would be another one before they left. However, as she made her way to her own tent and got ready for bed, she was very aware that they wouldn't be in Honduras for much longer. Another day—two at the most—and that would be it: there would be no hope of finding any more casualties after that so they would pack up and return to England. And once they were home that would be the end for her and

Rafferty. They would go their separate ways and there was nothing she could do to stop it happening.

She took a deep breath when she felt tears burn her eyes. Crying wouldn't help to salvage their relationship. She had to convince him that he could trust her enough to unlock his emotions, but she could only do that if he truly loved her.

She sighed because she'd come full circle and was right back where she'd started—wondering if Rafferty loved her enough to want to spend his life with her.

CHAPTER TEN

'THE instruments will need to be packed into those foam-lined cases before they're put inside the crates. There's a customs declaration form that will need to be filled out as well so I'll do that before we load them onto the trucks.'

Rafferty made a note on the increasingly long list of jobs that still needed doing, then carried on. They were in the process of dismantling the camp and there was a lot to get through if they were to be ready to set off at midday. They were booked onto a flight that left Comayagua Palmerola airport at eight that night and it would take them at least five hours to drive to the airport so he had to make sure that they kept to a very strict timetable.

The search-and-rescue teams were also leaving. They had stopped digging the previous night when it had been decided that there was no hope of finding any more survivors in the rubble, and they were now packing up their equipment. It had been an international effort with teams on site from the USA, the UK and France, as well as from several neighbouring South American countries. He glanced up when the clatter of helicopter rotors overhead announced that one of the teams was on its way. Soon everyone would have left and the local people would have to try and get their lives back into some semblance of order.

Wally, the head of their ground crew, came over to speak to him just then about some problems they were having with dismantling the theatre tent so Rafferty went to see what was wrong. It turned out that one of the main supporting struts had become jammed into place and no amount of pushing and pulling would budge it.

In the end he agreed that the support would have to be cut so the tent could be dismantled, but he was aware that it was going to put the crew under extra pressure to get packed away on time. It was the last thing he needed, too, because he didn't feel up to dealing with any more problems. He had enough to contend with, thinking about him and Natalie, without adding to his stress levels. Had he done the right thing by telling her that they should split up, or should he reconsider his decision?

'All the nursing supplies are packed now—dressings, linens, etcetera—so what else needs doing?'

He glanced round when the subject of his thoughts suddenly materialised at his side, feeling his heart kick up a storm. Just being near her was enough to make his body go into overdrive. She was dressed in jeans and a ratty old sweater because it was messy work, packing everything away, but she still managed to look utterly desirable and gorgeous.

She could wear a bin liner and he'd still want her, Rafferty thought wistfully. It was just the kind of thought he could have done without when he was experiencing doubts about the wisdom of his decision. He'd done what was right for Natalie and that was what mattered!

'Can you check on the last few patients who are still here?' he asked gruffly. 'Dilia Meléndez is being transferred to the main hospital at Tegucigalpa and I want to make sure the consultant there understands exactly what's happened to her. It will be touch and go whether she survives now that infection has set in.'

'Patsy is translating Dilia's notes into Spanish to make sure the staff at the hospital know what treatment she's been on.' Natalie sighed. 'It doesn't seem fair that she's got this far and might not pull through.'

'It's really tough on her family. I spoke to her husband yesterday and he was beside himself with worry,' Rafferty agreed sadly. 'Let's hope the new antibiotic regime she's on will have a beneficial effect over the next day or so. Anyway, thank Patsy for me, will you? It's good of her to go to all that extra trouble.'

'All part of the service,' Natalie said lightly, and he grimaced.

'I know. And if it's any consolation, I've apologised to Patsy for my remarks the other day.'

'So she said. Right, I'll check on Dilia then make sure the rest of the patients are ready for when the ambulances arrive.' She broke off when Joanna suddenly came rushing over to them.

'We've just received a radio message to say that a helicopter has crashed in the mountains not far from here,' Joanna announced, breathless after her dash across the compound. 'It's the chopper that was due to ferry the S and R team back to Florida.'

'Do they know if there's any survivors?' Rafferty bit out.

'Yes. The pilot managed to radio through to base. They're all injured, apparently, but it's the copilot who's come off worst. Air traffic control at Miami have contacted the relevant authorities but they want to know if we're in a position to respond until they get here.'

'They want us to give the crew medical assistance?' Rafferty clarified, frowning when Joanna nodded. 'If we can get to them, of course we'll help, but where exactly are they?'

'I'm not sure. Larry has been liaising with the guys at air traffic control. He was still trying to get a fix on the crew's location when I came to find you.'

'Right. The best thing to do is find out where exactly they've come down and take it from there.' Rafferty handed Joanna the clipboard. 'Can you take over here while I check what's going on?'

'Of course.'

Joanna took the clipboard while he and Natalie went to

find Larry. He was in the small tent they used as their communications centre. He looked up when they went in but he was busily talking to someone from air traffic control. Rafferty waited with mounting impatience while the other man wrote down a series of map co-ordinates.

'So do we have a fix on them yet?' he demanded as soon as Larry ended the call.

'Here you go.' Larry handed him the co-ordinates then pulled out a detailed map of the area. 'Let's see if we can pinpoint their location from this.'

Rafferty read out the co-ordinates while Larry cross-referenced them against the map, his heart sinking when he saw where the helicopter had crashed. 'It's halfway up a mountain.'

'I know. How on earth are we going to get up there to help them?' Larry replied worriedly.

Rafferty frowned as he studied the contours printed on the map. 'They must have come down at roughly eight thousand feet from the look of it. It will take us ages if we have to climb up there to reach them, always assuming we can manage to climb that far, of course, and there's no guarantee about that. The mountains around here are very steep and we're not equipped for an operation like that. What we really need is someone to drop us off on the mountain as near as possible to where the chopper came down.'

'One of the other helicopters, you mean,' Natalie put in, and he stifled a sigh because he really didn't need any more reminders about how quickly she'd always followed his train of thought. When it came to such matters they were in complete harmony—unlike other areas of their life.

'Yes,' he replied with as much equanimity as he could muster in the circumstances. 'If we can get one of the pilots to drop us off, it will save us a lot of valuable time. If the copilot is as badly injured as they say he is, every extra minute counts.'

'I'll go over to the search-and-rescue camp and see if I can find someone to help us,' she offered at once. 'A lot of the teams are still packing up and I'm sure someone will offer their services once they find out what's happened.'

'And while you're doing that, I'll sort out our equipment.' Rafferty grimaced. 'Isn't it typical that we're going to need some of our stuff when we've only just packed it away?'

'I'll give you a hand,' Larry offered, following them out of the tent.

Rafferty left Natalie to sort out their transport arrangements while he and Larry went over to the trucks, which were in the process of being loaded with their equipment. He quickly explained to the others what had happened and in a very short time they'd managed to put together some packs of medical supplies. Natalie came back just as they were finishing packing everything into a couple of haversacks, and he glanced up at her.

'Well?'

'Everyone wanted to help but a lot of the teams are travelling out by road then flying home from the airport. In the end, it was decided that the Nicaraguan pilot would ferry us over there in his helicopter. He's ready to leave whenever you say the word.'

'Good.' Rafferty stood up and looked around the assembled group, knowing that it was going to cause a lot of problems if the whole team was delayed. Their seats on the plane were booked and paid for: there was no way that he could justify the expense of cancelling them when it would cost the agency such a lot of money.

'It will cause too many problems if we delay our departure so I want the rest of you to carry on as we've arranged. I've no idea how long it's going to take us to find those guys, neither do I have any idea what state they'll be in when we get to them, so just Natalie and I will go. We'll try to catch up with you at the airport but we might need to reschedule our flights home if we're delayed for too long.'

There was a bit of muttering because the rest of the team were obviously loath to leave without them. However, in the end they saw the wisdom of what he was saying. Rafferty handed over the customs forms and other documents to Larry and asked him to liaise with Joanna, then turned to Natalie.

'We'd better get a move on. The sooner we find those guys, the better it will be for everyone concerned.'

Natalie nodded as she picked up a haversack. 'The helicopter is over here,' she told him briefly, leading the way.

Rafferty picked up the other pack and waved when the rest of the team wished them good luck. The helicopter pilot, Efraín Molina, was waiting beside his machine so Rafferty wasted no time as he introduced himself and climbed on board. The pilot and the winchman ran through the preflight checks while he and Natalie strapped themselves in.

Rafferty glanced at her as they lifted off a few minutes later and felt a rush of happiness suddenly fill him. The next few hours would be a testing time for them both, but having Natalie with him made him feel as though he could overcome any obstacles. She gave him confidence and strength, empowered him just by her presence. She meant the whole world to him and even though he knew that they had to part when they got back to England, at least he would have this time with her to look back on.

Natalie could feel her tension rising as the helicopter swooped over the mountains. All around them the jagged peaks soared towards the sky. They had flown over oak and pine forests but the vegetation had thinned out as they'd travelled deeper into the mountain range. Now just a few sparse trees hugged the rocky ground below them.

'We must be nearly there by now.'

Rafferty's voice echoed tinnily through her headset and

she turned towards him, feeling her heart ache with a fierce pain when she saw the warmth in his beautiful green eyes. If only it was there because of her, she thought wistfully, but there was no point in deluding herself. He was eager to get this rescue under way, excited by the prospect of saving lives under the most arduous conditions. It was what made him tick, what made his life mean something, and she mustn't make the mistake of thinking that it was her presence that had made him look so animated.

'The pilot said it would take us about fifteen minutes to reach them, didn't he?' she replied, deliberately removing any trace of emotion from her voice.

'It's just about that now so we should see some sign of them pretty soon—' He broke off and pointed to a spot below them. 'That's them. There.'

Natalie turned and stared out of the window, her stomach churning when she saw the crumpled remains of the helicopter far below. It was about halfway up the side of the mountain and she had no idea how they were going to get to it because the ground looked very steep, from what she could see. The pilot's voice suddenly came through her headset, advising them that he was going to fly over the area again to see if he could find somewhere to land. She held her breath as the helicopter swooped round in a wide circle then started to lose height. She had a better view of the area now and her heart sank as it became obvious that the slope was too steep for them to land.

'There's got to be some way of getting down there.' Rafferty's tone echoed her frustration as he studied the rough terrain, and Natalie sighed.

'There's just nowhere to set down, is there? It's much too steep.'

'No, we can't land, but we could be winched down.'

'Winched down!' she repeated in horror. 'You have to be

joking. I've never been winched out of a helicopter before. Have you?'

'Nope. But there's a first time for everything, isn't there?' He suddenly grinned at her. 'We've come *this* far, so we can't just give up at the first hurdle, can we?'

'Some hurdle,' she muttered darkly.

'It can't be that difficult, Natalie. People get winched out of helicopters every day of the week.' His tone softened, took on a cajoling note that made her grit her teeth because she knew to her cost how effective it could be. 'You'll be perfectly safe. Honest.'

'I'll never hear the end of it if I refuse, will I?' she said with a sigh, because there was no point trying to hold out. When Rafferty turned on the charm she was putty in his hands…as he undoubtedly knew!

'Thanks.' He touched her lightly on the hand and she felt her nerves flicker in response when she felt the warmth of his skin on hers. It was a relief when he let her go so he could position the tiny microphone attached to his helmet closer to his mouth while he spoke to the pilot.

Natalie waited in silence while the two men had a brief discussion about the logistics of what they were proposing to do. There wasn't any point her chipping in, because she would go along with whatever he decided. She would trust him with her life and the thought was almost too poignant in the circumstances, because once they returned to England he would no longer be there when she needed him to help and encourage her. He would no longer be there to drive her mad with his stubbornness, just as he would no longer be there to hold her in his arms and make her feel more alive than any woman had ever felt before. He would be gone from her life for good and she didn't think she could bear it. She didn't want to try!

'Rafferty—'

'They're going to winch us down over there.' He was all

business as he turned to her again. 'Then we'll just have to climb the last few feet to reach the crew.'

'Will they be able to winch the injured men back up into the helicopter?' she asked dully, because once again the moment had passed her by.

'They're not equipped for that kind of operation, I'm afraid. Efraín's spoken to air traffic control and they're sending a fully equipped Medivac rescue helicopter to pick up the casualties. We'll just do what we can until it gets here.'

'Fine.'

Natalie didn't ask him any more questions because it was pointless to waste time. When the winchman tapped her on the shoulder and beckoned her to follow him to the bay doors, she unfastened her seat belt and got up. She waited while he fitted her and Rafferty with safety harnesses then explained how they undid the bolts that would secure them to the line when they were winched to the ground. Rafferty had decided to go first so he could help her, so she moved aside while the doors were opened, sucking in her breath as the wind rushed into the cabin. The ground looked an awfully long way away from where they were standing and she gulped at the thought of dangling off a thin little cable while she was lowered down to the mountainside.

'You'll be fine.' Rafferty smiled at her and she tried her best to smile back but some of the trepidation she was feeling obviously showed on her face. He pulled her to him and hugged her hard and she heard the sudden roughness in his voice.

'I won't let anything bad happen to you, Natalie.'

Emotion welled up inside her so that it was hard to smile back at him when she felt so choked up. 'I know you won't,' she said huskily.

'Do you?'

The urgency in his voice was impossible to ignore, even

though she wasn't sure what it meant. 'I would trust you with my life,' she said simply, because it was true.

Something crossed his face, an emotion so raw that her breath caught. It was as though for the first time ever he'd completely lowered his guard and allowed her a glimpse of the real man behind the highly controlled exterior, but before she could say anything, he turned away.

Natalie's hand clenched as she watched him step out onto one of the skids. Her heart was pounding as she watched the ground rushing up towards them until she was sure they would crash as well. Then at the very last second the pilot levelled off. The winchman tapped Rafferty on the shoulder and the next second he disappeared from sight.

She looked down, watching in terror as he was lowered on the end of the cable. It only took a couple of seconds before he reached the ground. He released the clasp on his harness and the winchman reeled the line back in and attached it to her harness.

Natalie could feel her legs trembling as she stepped out onto the narrow metal skid. The winchman suddenly tapped her on the shoulder and she closed her eyes and folded her arms, as she'd been instructed to do, as she stepped off onto fresh air. The wind rushed around her, buffeting her sideways as she spun towards the ground. She gasped in terror but the next moment Rafferty had hold of her. He sat her down on a rock while he unfastened the cable from her harness, grinning broadly when she finally managed to peel her eyelids apart.

'Fun, wasn't it?' he teased, and she glared at him.

'It might be your idea of fun but it certainly wasn't mine!'

'Oh, come on, Natalie, I could tell you were having the time of your life.'

'Could you indeed? Then all I can say is that it's no wonder we never agree on anything,' she replied testily, because she still felt very wobbly after her descent from the skies. 'Obviously, you don't know me very well, Rafferty!'

His face closed up as he rose and held the cable away from them so the winchman could reel it in. 'Then it's a good job that we've seen sense at last and called it a day, isn't it?'

Natalie bit her lip, wishing with all her heart that she hadn't said that, especially after the way he'd seemed to open up to her in the helicopter. She longed to apologise but she could tell from his set expression that he wouldn't listen to her.

She stood up as Rafferty finished unclipping their haversacks from the cable. The winchman reeled in the line for the last time and the helicopter lifted off, the downdraught from its rotors almost blasting them off the side of the mountain. Rafferty grabbed hold of her arm and his touch was so impersonal that she could have wept, only it wouldn't have achieved anything. When he handed her one of the rucksacks, she took it without a word. There was nothing to say that hadn't been said before. They'd quarrelled and apologised so many times that it had become routine, yet not once had they addressed the reasons for their problems, and she blamed herself for that.

She should have realised sooner the effect Rafferty's upbringing must have had on him, instead of dismissing his concerns. Now it was too late to redress the damage, too late to do anything except go along with this decision he'd made that they must part. She could tell him that she understood his fears, but she couldn't take them away from him and she'd never felt more helpless in her life. She didn't want to lose him but she simply didn't know how to keep him either!

'Am I glad to see you guys!'

Rafferty dredged up a smile as they crested the final ridge and found themselves face to face with the pilot of the stricken helicopter. The climb had been far more arduous than he'd expected it would be and he'd been worried in case it had been too much for Natalie. A couple of times he'd been tempted to tell her to wait while he found an easier route but he'd guessed what sort of response he would get. Natalie didn't need his help—as she'd made abundantly clear.

'I bet you are.' He held out his hand, reminding himself that it was pointless torturing himself now when he would have years to think about the fact that Natalie didn't need him. 'I'm Michael Rafferty, one of the surgeons with Worlds Together. Miami air traffic control asked us to pop up here and see if we could stick on a plaster or two.'

'Tom Wolfe. Although I'm none too sure what a plaster is, I'm happy to let you do whatever you like so long as you start with Dex.' Tom glanced over to where the other two crew members were lying and lowered his voice. 'He's in a pretty bad way, from what I can tell, Doc.'

'Then I'll check him over first.' Rafferty turned to Natalie, making sure that no trace of emotion was in his voice. 'Can you take a look at Tom while I check on the copilot?'

'Of course.' She dropped her backpack on the ground and smiled at the pilot. 'I'm Natalie Palmer and I'm a nurse-practitioner so you can safely let me stick on your BAND-AID, which I believe is what you call them in the US.'

'So that's what they are. Shame. I was hoping it might involve a rather more *intimate* procedure, seeing as I'm going to be in your tender care.'

Rafferty turned away as she laughed, because it wasn't very professional to want to punch a patient on the nose. Neither was it his place to object to the tone of the banter either. He'd given up any right to have a say in her life so he would have to get used to watching other men flirt with her.

It was a depressing thought, so he tried not to dwell on it

as he made his way over to where the copilot was lying. He was conscious but obviously in a bad way. He managed to tell Rafferty that his name was Jeff Dexter—Dex to his friends—but even that brief conversation proved too much and he passed out before Rafferty finished examining him.

Rafferty's spirits plummeted further as he logged up a broken leg and a displaced collar-bone, as well as fractures to both arms. It certainly wouldn't be easy to get the man down from the mountain in this state. He was just checking Dex's spine when Natalie arrived and crouched down beside him.

'The pilot seems to have had a miraculous escape. He's got a sprained wrist and a couple of cuts on his right forearm, but nothing serious.'

'Good. That's one less to worry about. Could you check the winchman next?' Rafferty barely glanced up because he was too busy checking the copilot's spine. 'He looks a bit disorientated so he might have bumped his head when they crashed.'

'Will do.'

She got up and went over to the other man while Rafferty finished what he was doing. His searching fingers suddenly detected a misalignment in the cervical spine and he groaned—it was the worst possible place for an injury. Damage to the spinal cord at this point could result in quadriplegia—paralysis in all four limbs—so his main concern now was to minimise the risk of any further damage occurring.

He took a cervical collar out of his bag and fitted it around the copilot's neck, then found a head restraint, using a length of tape across the man's forehead as an added security measure to prevent him moving. Inflatable splints on his arms and leg helped to stabilise them but there was little Rafferty could do about his collar-bone, because he couldn't risk moving him while he manipulated it back into place. They would have to sort it out at the hospital, so he left it at that. Natalie came back as he was administering a shot of morphine for the pain and he could tell at once that she was worried.

'The winchman's definitely suffered a head trauma. I'd guess there's subdural bleeding because he seems very disorientated and he's also slurring his words. I'd put his GCS at about seven.'

'He needs to be admitted to hospital if we're to avert a disaster,' he said bluntly. 'The same goes for this fellow. Slide your hand under here and tell me what you can feel.'

He moved aside so she could check the patient's spine, seeing the worry on her face when she looked up. 'Definite misalignment between C5 and C6,' she confirmed.

'Which means we'll need to handle him with kid gloves when we have to move him.' Rafferty took a deep breath, forcing himself to focus on what needed to be done for their patients. It wasn't easy when his thoughts kept wandering back to Natalie all the time, but he had to do what was right. 'We need to keep a close watch on the winchman as well as the copilot, check if there's any change in his condition—fitting, loss of consciousness—you know the drill.'

'Fine. I'll stay with him while you keep an eye on the copilot. Is there anything else we can do for him?'

'I'm going to set up a drip. With this level of injury, shock is going to be a problem, although the biggest problem of all will be getting him off the mountain.'

He broke off as the radio in his backpack suddenly started crackling. He depressed the receive button and was surprised when he recognised Larry's voice on the other end of the line.

'What's wrong?' he asked, because he could only assume there must be a problem if Larry had contacted him. The team should have been on their way to the airport by now and he couldn't imagine why they were still at the camp. 'I thought you'd have left by now.'

'We were just about to set off when Miami control got

onto us again so I stayed back to contact you. Apparently, there's a hitch with the rescue helicopter. They've forecast dense cloud over the mountains and the chopper won't be able to fly out until it clears.'

'We have two men here in urgent need of medical treatment,' Rafferty bit out. 'We're talking about a major head trauma as well as an unstable spinal injury.'

'Then I don't know what to suggest for the best. I'll get back onto Miami and explain how urgent the situation is, but they weren't very hopeful a few minutes ago when I spoke to them.'

'Do that. And tell them that we need help and we need it sooner rather than later if we're to avert a double tragedy.' Rafferty put the radio back in the bag, sighing when he saw the worry on Natalie's face. 'It never rains but it pours, does it?'

'What's happened now?'

'They've forecast dense cloud over the mountains and the rescue helicopter doesn't know when it will be able to get here.'

'No! But what are we going to do in the meantime?'

'I've no idea. We need that helicopter, because there is no way we can carry these men down the mountainside.'

'Maybe they'll send someone up here on foot to help us,' she suggested.

'Maybe.' He shrugged, deeming it wiser not to point out how long it would take a team of mountaineers to reach them. There was no point piling on the pressure and making it even more stressful for her.

He stood up abruptly, suddenly wishing that he hadn't involved her in the first place. He knew how upset she would be if they lost the two men and he blamed himself for not thinking about that before. His tone was gruff when he continued, because the last thing he wanted was to cause her any more unhappiness.

'Can you keep an eye on the copilot while I take a look at the other guy? I'd just like to assess for myself how bad he is.'

'Of course.'

They traded places and Rafferty went over to the winchman. Tom was with him and he looked up when Rafferty appeared.

'Jim's not looking too good, Doc.'

Rafferty nodded as he squatted down beside the injured man. His eyes were closed and he was muttering under his breath. He quickly checked the man's skull, his heart sinking when he felt a deep depression above the winchman's right ear.

'It looks as though there could be bleeding going on inside his skull,' he told Tom flatly.

'They'll be able to sort it out at the hospital, though?' the pilot asked hopefully.

'Yes, but we're not sure when we'll be able to get him to hospital.'

He quickly explained their predicament and the pilot nodded.

'You can't fly a helicopter in dense cloud. It's way too risky in a mountainous region like this. I've flown in this area before and once the cloud sets in, it can be days before it lifts.'

'It will be too late by then, I'm afraid.'

Rafferty came to a sudden decision, knowing that he didn't have a choice. The winchman's condition was deteriorating rapidly and if he didn't do something soon the man would die. He stood up and went back to Natalie, knowing that what he was suggesting was extremely risky. However, it might be the only chance the man had.

'I'm going to do a craniotomy. He's getting worse and we can't afford to wait for an unspecified length of time until the helicopter gets here.'

'A craniotomy?' she echoed in astonishment.

'We don't have a choice, Natalie. There's pressure building up inside his skull and we need to release it. We've got everything we need, apart from a drill,' he continued as calmly as he could. Performing such a delicate procedure on the side of a mountain would be a new experience even for him.

'Maybe the pilot has one. They usually keep a fairly comprehensive tool kit on most aircraft.'

Rafferty's brows rose steeply. 'And where did you glean that little nugget of information from?'

'From the company's pilot.'

She looked him straight in the eyes and he knew that she was waiting for him to make some sort of remark. He sighed under his breath because it didn't make him feel good to realise how childishly he'd behaved. All those comments he'd made hadn't helped and he bitterly regretted them.

He'd always felt uncomfortable about the difference in their lifestyles yet what did it really matter when it came down to it? So what if Natalie's family was rich? And so what if she'd been brought up with every conceivable kind of luxury and he'd had to work for everything he had? Did it really change who they were inside?

The thought stunned him. It was as though a light had been switched on and he could see the situation clearly for the first time—see how foolish he'd been to think that any of those things had mattered. He loved Natalie, not despite her wealth or because of it. He loved her for herself—for the warm, caring, sexy, desirable woman she was—and there was no reason to believe that she didn't love him for who *he* was either.

He groaned in despair. Why in the name of all that was holy hadn't he realised it sooner?

CHAPTER ELEVEN

'HOLD him steady…that's fine. I just need to drill this last hole then we can see what we're dealing with.'

Natalie held her breath as Rafferty drilled the final burr hole in the man's skull. The operation was a delicate one at the best of times, and under present conditions she knew how dangerous it was. However, she wasn't in any doubt about what they were doing. Unless they managed to relieve the pressure inside the winchman's skull, he would die.

'Just as we suspected.' Rafferty's tone held a certain grim satisfaction when he removed the lid of bone to reveal a massive haematoma.

'It's huge!' Natalie exclaimed.

'One of the biggest I've ever seen.' He smiled wryly. 'We should have known it would be. It's always the way, isn't it? These things never happen when you've got access to a nice, safe, sterile theatre unit.'

She chuckled at that. 'Yes, it's typical, isn't it? The one time you decide to perform a craniotomy alfresco it turns out to be a monster haematoma you're dealing with.'

Rafferty laughed. 'It's certainly that all right.'

He returned his attention to the patient, working with his usual skill and dexterity despite the unusual circumstances, and Natalie felt a huge wave of pride well up inside her as she watched him. Other surgeons would have balked at attempting this kind of surgery under such difficult conditions but not Rafferty. He was bold when he needed to be, yet ultra-careful when it was essential that he should proceed with caution. He seemed able to respond no matter how difficult the situation was, in fact.

Was that because of his childhood? she wondered suddenly, and just as suddenly knew it was so. He had learned from an early age to rely on his own judgement, to take decisions and stick to them no matter what the consequences might be. Her heart ached at the thought because it proved how hard it would be to persuade him to change his mind about them.

'That's got rid of it.' He suddenly looked up and she quickly returned her attention to where it should have remained all along—with their patient.

'Are you going to close up now?' she asked, steadying the patient's head as Rafferty began replacing the section of bone he'd removed from the man's skull.

'Yes. The sooner everything is back in place the better, wouldn't you say?' He deftly stitched the membranes, muscles and skin back into place then sat back on his heels and stretched. 'Shame they don't make a portable operating table. Crouching down like this is extremely hard on the thigh muscles.'

'Maybe you could come up with a suitable design,' she suggested drolly, covering the wound with a layer of sterile gauze.

'Then I could patent it and make my fortune?' He shook his head. 'Can't see it being a big seller, can you?'

'Not unless there are other crazy surgeons out there prepared to operate on the side of a mountain or somewhere similar. And somehow I don't think there are that many about.' She shot him a teasing look. 'I rather think they broke the mould after they made you, Michael Rafferty. You're one of a kind!'

'I'm not sure how to take that,' he replied, grinning at her, and her heart caught when she saw the warmth in his eyes.

'You should take it as a compliment,' she said softly, holding his gaze. 'Because that's how it was meant.'

Something crossed his face, an expression of such yearning that her breath caught. 'Even after the way I've behaved in the last few days?'

'You aren't the only one to blame. I've behaved very foolishly, too.'

She bit her lip when she felt tears well into her eyes but she didn't want to stop now that she finally had the opportunity to tell him how sorry she was for not understanding his fears sooner. 'You kept trying to explain how you felt about my family and everything, but I wouldn't listen, would I?'

'I never meant to hurt you, sweetheart,' he said gently.

'I know that. I was just so…so *set* on seeing the situation from my side. I should have realised that your background was bound to have had an effect on you and that there were issues we needed to discuss.'

'And now you understand what I was getting at?' he said tersely, and she frowned when she heard the edge in his voice.

'I think so.' She paused, hoping he would say something else, but he just sat there, his face like stone as he waited for her to continue.

Natalie wet her lips, wondering why she felt so nervous all of a sudden. She just wanted to clear up this misunderstanding so they could find a way forward that wouldn't entail them splitting up. However, her voice sounded oddly hesitant when she carried on and it was the last thing she wanted when she needed to sound full of confidence to convince him.

'Your childhood was the antithesis of mine. Oh, I know that you've always skirted around the subject whenever it's cropped up, but I can read between the lines. That's why you've always been so conscious of the difference in our lifestyles, and maybe you were right to be aware of them, too.'

'It would be foolish not to take it into account,' he agreed, and the flatness of his voice made a shiver run through her even though she couldn't explain why it alarmed her so much.

'It would,' she said quickly, wanting to get the conversation over. Once she'd explained that she understood, there wouldn't be a problem, she reasoned. All it needed was for them to be truthful with each other and they could resolve this issue. 'You can't just discount my upbringing, just as I can't discount yours. It's part of who we are.'

'And you are the daughter of a millionaire and I'm the product of my own efforts. Yes, I'm very aware of who we are, Natalie. Believe me.'

He stood up abruptly. 'Anyway, enough of all that. I need to check on the copilot. Can you keep an eye on the winchman? I'm not expecting any problems but you never know in a case like this. I'll also try to get hold of Larry again and see if there's been any developments with that helicopter.'

'Of course,' Natalie murmured, somewhat stunned by the speed with which he'd brought the conversation to an end. Had he just been worried about their patients? she wondered as she watched him walk over to the copilot. Or had there been another reason why he'd not wanted to talk about his past any more?

She sighed. It was obviously the latter. He still felt deeply uncomfortable talking about his childhood and it was worrying to know that she'd not had time to reassure him that it was the person he was today she cared about. She would have felt happier if she'd managed to make that clear to him but she could tell him how she felt as soon as he came back.

She smiled as she bent and checked her patient's pulse. Telling Rafferty that she loved him was going to be the best thing she'd done in a very long time…

'Thanks, Larry. It's a real weight off my mind to know that we'll be out of here fairly soon.'

Rafferty switched off the radio. Apparently, the cloud

cover had started to lift and the Medivac chopper would be with them within the hour. Once they handed over the casualties, the helicopter that had flown them there would collect them and ferry them to Comayagua Palmerola airport, where they would be able to rejoin the rest of the team. Everything had worked out surprisingly well in the end—if he discounted that conversation he'd had with Natalie just now.

His mouth compressed as he went to tell her that they would be leaving shortly. He couldn't begin to explain how painful he'd found it to hear her admit that his background did make a difference to her. Maybe he should be glad that she'd faced up to the truth at last, but it was hard to feel anything positive in the circumstances. The woman he loved had realised that he wasn't the man she wanted to spend her life with, and it hurt. It hurt like hell!

'Everything all right?'

Rafferty struggled to contain his emotions when she looked round as he approached, because the last thing he wanted was to play upon her sympathies. She would be upset if she realised that he'd been hurt by her reaction and he refused to do anything that might make her reconsider her position. If he didn't measure up to her requirements, he just had to accept that.

'The cloud cover has started to lift so the Medivac helicopter should be here within the hour,' he explained tersely.

Crouching down, he took a torch out of his pocket and checked the injured man's response to light because it was easier to think about work than the fact that his heart was breaking. The man's pupils reacted when he shone the light into them—a positive sign that the operation had been a success—so at least some good had come out of this, he thought grimly as he switched off the torch.

'That's a relief. I had visions of us being stuck on the side of this mountain all day!' She smiled at him, her beautiful face alight with laughter, and the pain that was gnawing away inside him intensified until he couldn't stand it any longer.

'No danger of that now,' he said coldly. It was the only way he could cope with what was happening. If he allowed his emotions to surface, he had no idea what would happen, and the thought scared him half to death. Begging her to love him the way he loved her wasn't an option if he hoped to salvage a shred of self-respect from this whole sorry episode.

'You'll be back in civilisation very soon so you won't have to put up with any more discomfort.'

Her smile faded abruptly when she heard the chill in his voice. 'Meaning what exactly?'

'Meaning that you really aren't cut out for this kind of work, are you, Natalie? You're more a glitz-and-glamour sort of woman, someone who enjoys the comforts in life.'

He rocked back on his heels and treated her to a condescending smile, wondering when he'd become such a good liar. These weren't his words coming out of his mouth—not the words he *wanted* to say—but they were the only ones he could come up with if he was to do what was right. And severing the last ties that bound Natalie to him was the right thing to do.

'Am I, indeed? So that's how you see me, is it? As someone who needs the good things in life to be happy?'

Her voice held an answering chill but it didn't disguise the pain it held as well, and Rafferty's heart shrivelled up inside him when he realised how much he'd hurt her. He was sorely tempted to apologise at that point, only he couldn't do that. He had to set her free so that she could get on with her life—without him dragging her down.

'Mmm. Don't get me wrong—you've always done a first-rate job whenever we've been away on a mission. But now I've had time to see how you operate in your own world and it's really opened my eyes, I have to admit.' He shrugged. 'You're far more at home in the cut and thrust of business and I was wrong to suggest that you should rethink what you've been doing recently. You should carry on running Palmer's because it's obvious that it's what you do best.'

He spread his hands wide apart, taking in the stark landscape. 'This isn't the right environment for you, Natalie. Really it isn't. So go back home to London and stop trying to do a job you really aren't suited for.'

Natalie let herself into her house and tossed her keys onto the console table by the front door. Dropping her haversack onto the floor, she deactivated the alarm, sighing in relief when she heard the mechanical beeps that indicated the code had been accepted. The last thing she needed was half a dozen security guards hammering on the door to check if she was all right, because what would she tell them? That her heart was broken and her whole life was in a mess because the man she loved didn't want anything more to do with her?

Tears welled into her eyes but she dashed them away. She hadn't cried once on the journey back from Honduras and she refused to start crying now. Fortunately, the hours since they had handed over the casualties to the Medivac crew had been too hectic to think about what had happened on that mountainside. As soon as the Medivac chopper had flown away, they'd been picked up and ferried to the airport where the rest of the team had been waiting for them.

Everyone had wanted to hear what had happened so she'd given them a blow-by-blow account, hyping up the danger and the drama in a way she wouldn't normally have done. She could tell that Rafferty had been surprised by her effusiveness but she'd ignored him, determined to keep on talking for as long as possible because it was the best way she knew to stop herself thinking about what he'd said.

How could he have claimed that she wasn't suited to the work Worlds Together did? How could he even *think* that she'd be happier living a pampered life in the city? Did he really know so little about her? Obviously he must, and it hurt to know how stupid she'd been to imagine that he had ever truly loved her. If Rafferty had felt anything akin to love for her, he would have known the kind of person she was!

A sob rose to her throat but she swallowed it down as she made her way to the kitchen and plugged in the kettle. She was parched after the long flight because she'd refused the on-board refreshments, too concerned in case she'd thrown up to risk eating or drinking anything. Opening the refrigerator, she took out a carton of milk, grimacing when she unscrewed the cap and discovered that it had gone sour. She would have to drink her coffee black because she was far too tired to go to the shops and buy some more.

She spooned instant coffee into a mug and topped it up with boiling water then took it into the sitting room and sat down. The house smelt musty after being shut up for over a week, but she couldn't summon the energy to open the windows. She drank her coffee then rested her head against the cushion and dozed for a while, but even though she was exhausted, she was too keyed up to sleep properly.

Opening her eyes, she checked her watch and realised with a pang that it was only a little after nine a.m. The thought of sitting in the house all day, brooding about what had happened, was more than she could face so she decided to go to the office. So long as she kept busy, she wouldn't need to think about Rafferty, and if she didn't think about him, it would get easier in time. People said that time was a great healer, so she would test out the theory. However, as she made her way upstairs to get changed, she knew in her heart that time wasn't going to help in this instance. The more time she spent apart from Rafferty, the more she was going to miss him.

Rafferty went straight home after they landed at Heathrow and packed an overnight bag with some clean clothes. He didn't even stop to shower or change before he left again and went out to his car. Maybe it was cowardly to run away but he didn't know what else he could do. He needed to get out of London and away from Natalie, otherwise who knew what he might be tempted to do?

He started the engine with a throaty roar that seemed to sum up his feelings perfectly. He felt like roaring, too—roaring at fate for being so cruel as to make him fall in love with a woman whom he could never have, roaring because it wasn't *his* fault that he'd been abandoned as a child, roaring for all the good things that had ever happened in his life as well as the bad, because even the good didn't mean anything now.

What was the point of having a career he loved if Natalie wasn't there to share the highs and the lows with him? How could he celebrate because he'd achieved his dream of making a difference to people's lives when he couldn't do anything about his own life?

He'd never felt as bereft or as miserable as he did right then and the thought of having to endure years of feeling like that was almost too much to bear—only what else could he do? He'd burned his bridges, sent his beloved away in the hope that she would find someone worthy of her, and he couldn't go back on his decision. He couldn't and wouldn't do anything that might ruin Natalie's life!

He drove out of London, picking up speed once he was clear of the city. He had no idea where he was going because he wasn't going *to* any particular place but running away from somewhere he couldn't bear to be. The miles rolled by in a haze of despair until at last he arrived in Cumbria where he found a guest house with a vacancy sign in its window.

Rafferty went in and paid for a room, shrugging his shoulders when the owner asked how long he intended to stay. How long did it take to mend a broken heart? he wanted to reply but didn't, because it wasn't the sort of question a grown man asked a stranger. He went straight up to his room and lay down on the bed, and the minute he shut his eyes he saw Natalie—beautiful, loving, adorable Natalie.

Tears welled into his eyes and for the first time since he'd been a child he cried. He had lost the one person who had ever meant anything to him and he didn't know where he was going to go from this point on or how he was going to manage. Without Natalie in his life, he no longer knew who he really was.

'Hello, stranger! When did you get back?'

Natalie summoned a smile when Helen greeted her at the door of the clinic. It was just gone five and she'd gone straight there from the office. She knew that she should have gone home after she'd left Palmer's but the thought of spending the evening with only thoughts of Rafferty to keep her company had been more than she could bear. If she needed to fill every waking moment to get through this, that was what she would do. She wasn't a quitter—no matter what Rafferty thought about her.

The thought was too painful so she blanked it out of her mind as she followed Helen into the office. 'I got back this morning.'

'And you're going to work tonight?' Helen looked concerned as she sat down behind the desk. 'Are you sure you're up to it, Natalie? Don't get me wrong, we'd be really glad of the help because Annie is off sick at the moment, but it seems a bit much to expect you to work when you've only just got back.'

'I'm fine,' she insisted, slipping off her suit jacket. She hung it on the peg behind the door then took a plastic apron off the shelf and put it on over her silk blouse. 'I'm probably a bit jet-lagged after the flight so there's no point sitting at home when I won't be able to settle. My body still thinks it's on Honduras time.'

'Well, if you're sure you're OK?' Helen still sounded concerned.

Natalie smiled at her, forcing herself to appear upbeat so that her friend wouldn't suspect how dreadful she really felt. 'I feel fine. I'm raring to go, in fact.'

'In that case, thank heavens you're here.' Helen heaved a sigh as she sank back in the chair. 'It's been an absolute *nightmare* this past week, I can tell you.'

'Why? What's been happening?' Natalie asked in surprise, It wasn't like Helen to complain.

'We've had problems with a gang of youths who've been hanging around outside. They've been waylaying the kids and taking their prescriptions off them. It got so bad that in the end we had to call in the police, so that shows you how desperate we were.'

'Sounds really awful,' Natalie exclaimed in dismay. 'Did the police manage to sort things out?'

'Not really. Oh, the gang ran off when the police arrived but so did most of our kids as well. It took a couple of days before they started to come back to us so we're very wary about involving the police again. At the moment we're trying to monitor the situation by keeping an eye on what's going on outside the building.'

'I'm glad you warned me. I'll make sure there's nobody hanging around whenever I see someone out.'

'It's the only thing we can do, I'm afraid. It's a real catch-22 situation. If we involve the police, the kids who need our help stay away, and if we don't involve them they end up getting mugged for their prescriptions.' Helen shrugged. 'I don't know what the answer is, do you?'

'Maybe we could hire our own security guards,' she suggested, recalling what Rafferty had recommended when they'd had trouble once before with drunks. Her heart ached as the memory of that night came rushing back and she hurried on before the pain became too bad to bear. 'They wouldn't need to wear a uniform or anything official like that—just make their presence felt. That should be enough to deter the gang, I imagine.'

'It would be great if we could do that, but it's way too expensive to call in a private security firm. Our resources are stretched to the absolute limit as it is,' Helen pointed out sadly.

Natalie nodded. 'I know, but there might be a way around it. I've been working on a proposal to get some extra funding for the clinic from Palmer's charitable trust. Maybe we could cover the costs out of that?'

'That would be marvelous, but are you sure you want to do this for us, Natalie? I'd hate you to think that we're using you.'

'Of course you aren't using me! It was my idea in the first place so how can you say that?' She smiled at the other woman. 'Leave it with me and I'll see what I can do.'

Helen still looked a bit concerned so Natalie didn't pursue the idea. There was a bit of a rush shortly afterwards anyway, so they were both too busy to talk about it any more. Natalie checked each time she saw one of her patients out but the street was quiet each time, with no sign of anyone hanging about outside. She took a break at eight then worked until ten when all of a sudden exhaustion caught up with her. Helen must have noticed her yawning as she escorted her last patient from the treatment room because she came bustling over to her.

'OK, that's it,' she said firmly. 'You're to go home while you're still capable of walking.'

Natalie grimaced as another massive yawn caught up with her. 'I think you might be right. I'll just see Jessica out, then call it a night.'

She walked the girl to the door and smiled reassuringly at

her when the teenager hesitated. 'I'll watch until you reach the corner safely.'

'Thanks. One of the girls from the hostel had a bit of trouble the other night, which is why I didn't come to see you sooner. However, this rash has been driving me *crazy* so I decided I couldn't wait any longer.'

'Hopefully, this should clear it up.' Natalie glanced at the script she'd written for corticosteroid cream to combat an outbreak of dermatitis on the girl's arms caused by a reaction to the nickel in some bracelets Jessica had bought. 'You'll need to apply it for a few days, as I explained, but it should do the trick. Just make sure that you don't go buying any more jewellery unless you're certain that it's real gold next time.'

'Don't worry. I've learned my lesson. It's the last time I'll buy anything off a market stall!'

Jessica gave her a cheery wave then hurried up the street. Natalie watched until she reached the corner. She was just about to go back inside when she suddenly heard the girl scream. She didn't even pause to consider the wisdom of what she was doing as she raced out of the clinic and ran up the road. Rounding the corner, she ground to a halt when she found herself confronted by a gang of youths. Jessica was lying sprawled on the pavement with blood pouring down her cheek. One of the youths was standing over her, holding her prescription in his hand. It was obvious that he must have attacked her for it and Natalie saw red.

'What do you think you're doing?' she shouted, advancing towards him. She took another couple of steps then suddenly realised that another member of the gang had come up behind her.

She spun round then gasped when she felt something hit her in the chest. There was no pain, strangely enough, just the feel of the blow slamming into her body followed by the strangest sensation of not being able to breathe properly. She could hear Jessica screaming but the sound seemed to be coming from a long way away. Her vision started to blur and her last thought before she passed out was that she wished she'd told Rafferty how much she loved him.

CHAPTER TWELVE

RAFFERTY spent the rest of the day in his room, only leaving it when hunger forced him to go out and find something to eat. He drove to the nearest town and stopped at the first café he came to. It was packed with holidaymakers and he had to wait for a table but it didn't matter. He didn't have anything better to do so spending a few extra minutes hanging around wasn't important. Anyway, it helped fill in the time and that was what he needed to do most of all.

The waitress brought his meal and he ate everything on his plate even though he couldn't taste the food. He paid his bill then spent another hour wandering around the souvenir shops before he went back to the guest house. It was just gone seven but he got ready for bed because it was easier than trying to think of something else to fill in the time. It took him a while to fall asleep even though he was exhausted, and he was awake early the following morning but at least another few hours had passed, and if he joined all those hours together then maybe he'd get through the rest of his life somehow.

There were morning papers on the hall table when he went down for breakfast so he took one with him into the dining room to save him having to make conversation with the other guests. He ordered a full English breakfast because it would use up even more time while he ate it then opened the paper and skimmed through the usual stories of mayhem and bloodshed. It was only when he reached the centre pages that a half-inch column caught his attention and he froze when he read that a nurse working at a central London clinic for homeless teenagers had been stabbed the previous night.

Even though the paper didn't give any other details, he knew that it was Natalie they were referring to, Natalie who had been injured, Natalie who even now might be fighting for her life!

He flung the paper on the table and raced out of the room, ignoring the waitress who was in the process of bringing his breakfast. There was no time to explain where he was going, no time to do anything except get to Natalie. He would never forgive himself for not being there when she needed him, for allowing her to put herself in danger, for being so…so *pig-headed* about not telling her that he loved her. Maybe he couldn't have her in his life but he could have told her how he felt—that she was the most precious, the most wonderful thing that had ever happened to him. Now the thought that it might be too late to tell her that almost brought him to his knees—only he couldn't break down just yet, not until he'd seen her.

Afterwards, Rafferty remembered nothing of the drive back to London. He was on autopilot as the powerful car ate up the miles. It was lunchtime when he arrived and he drove straight to the hospital where the paper had said that she'd been taken, then had to endure a seemingly endless wait before the woman on duty at the reception desk informed him that, as he wasn't a relative, she couldn't give out any information about Miss Palmer.

'But that's ridiculous!' he stated, gripping the counter as a wave of fear threatened to engulf him, because there was only one reason he could think of why she was being so evasive. 'I demand to know which ward Miss Palmer is in.'

'I'm sorry, sir,' the receptionist replied primly. 'But it's a question of patient confidentiality—'

'Don't give me that!' he snapped, his patience eroded by the fear that was gnawing away inside him. Natalie couldn't be dead. She couldn't! 'If you won't tell me what I need to know, I demand to speak to someone who will!'

'If you carry on like that, sir, I shall have to ask you to leave.' The receptionist backed away from the counter and he cursed himself because he wasn't helping matters by losing his temper with her.

'I'm sorry. I didn't mean to shout at you but I've just driven halfway across the country and I'm worried sick.' He made a conscious effort to calm down. 'I'm a doctor so I do understand about patient confidentiality, but I really need to know if Miss Palmer is still here.'

'Well…' The receptionist wavered so Rafferty upped the ante by pulling out his hospital ID, at the same time treating her to his most winsome smile.

'Please. I'd be eternally grateful to you.'

'Well, I suppose it can't hurt if you're a doctor.' She suddenly caved in, obviously charmed into helping him. 'Miss Palmer is in ICU. That's on the sixth floor so you'll need to take the lift.'

Rafferty proffered his thanks as the woman directed him to the lifts on the far side of the reception area. He hurried towards them, feeling sick because Natalie's condition had to be extremely serious to warrant a precious intensive care bed. The ride up to the sixth floor was quick but he was seething with impatience by the time he got there. There was another reception desk outside the unit and he had to explain all over again who he was and who he wanted to see, not feeling in the least bit guilty about misleading the young receptionist on duty into thinking that he was a member of the hospital's staff. Every extra second's delay meant another second away from Natalie and he couldn't afford to waste any more time!

Natalie was in the bed nearest to the nurses' station. Rafferty's heart began to pound as he was taken through to see her because it was accepted practice to place the most seriously ill patients closest to the nurses. There was no point in deluding himself about what he was going to find but, even though he'd tried to prepare himself, the sight of her wired up to all the machinery still came as a shock.

His legs felt like jelly as he walked over to the bed and stood there, looking at her. Her face was ashen, her eyes closed, her chest rising and falling in the unnatural rhythm that resulted from having a machine breathing for her. Just twenty-four hours ago they'd knelt on that mountainside and saved a man's life; now here she was, looking as though her own life was ebbing away.

He sank to his knees, ignoring the nurse's murmur of astonishment as he grasped Natalie's hand. All the doubts he'd ever had, all the uncertainties that had plagued him no longer mattered. The only important thing was that she should live. Maybe they couldn't spend their lives together but so long as she didn't die and leave him, he would be happy. He simply couldn't imagine a world where Natalie was no longer a part of it and didn't want to try. It would be his own personal hell, a place of darkness and despair. He didn't have the strength to carry on without her.

There was a dull throbbing in her head and her throat hurt.

Natalie lay quite still for a moment, testing out these strange sensations that had invaded her body. She knew that she was in bed because she could tell that she was lying down, but it didn't feel like her bed. There was a heaviness about her limbs, too, that felt odd, almost as though she was being pinned down…

Her eyes flew open in panic and she stared in alarm at the array of machines lined up beside her. Monitors flickered, the brightly coloured lines, which were the visible signs of the various blips and beeps she could hear, hurting her eyes so that she closed them again then opened them when she realised that someone was speaking to her. The voice was familiar yet there was something odd about it, as though all that emotion it held was being contained only through a great deal of effort. Why on earth did Rafferty sound so upset? Had something awful happened?

She turned her head to look at him and felt her heart jolt in shock when she realised that he was crying. There were tears streaming down his face and the sight of them made her want to cry too, only her eyes felt horribly dry. A sob rose to her throat and she promptly started to gag because of the pain it caused her.

'Shh. Don't upset yourself now. It's all right, my darling. Everything is going to be fine.'

He bent and kissed her on the cheek, and his lips felt warm and damp when they touched her skin. Natalie wanted him to keep on kissing her because it felt so good, but all too quickly he drew back. She looked at him with eyes that mirrored her bewilderment and he smiled tenderly back at her.

'I know you must have lots of questions but you mustn't try to speak. Your throat will be swollen from having a tube in it.'

'Tube?' she croaked, screwing up her face in pain because it felt as though someone was sticking red-hot needles into her throat when she spoke.

'Yes. You've had the full works—tubes in and out all over the place and wires attaching you to all the monitors. The staff here could write a textbook about your blood pressure alone, I expect!'

She tried to respond to the teasing remark but she still had no real idea what was going on. Rafferty must have realised that she was confused because his grip on her hand tightened.

'You're in ICU, Natalie. You've been here for three days,' he explained gently. 'You were stabbed in the chest and your lungs collapsed, but you're going to be fine.'

'Stabbed,' she mouthed, not attempting to speak this time, partly through fear of the pain it would cause and partly out of shock.

'That's right. You were at the clinic when it happened.

You tried to help a girl who'd been attacked and someone stabbed you in the chest.'

Natalie gasped as she suddenly remembered her frantic dash along the road and the young girl sprawled across the pavement. 'Is she all right?' she whispered anxiously and Rafferty nodded.

'If you mean Jessica, she's fine. You don't need to worry about her—just concentrate on getting better.' He gently loosened his grip on her hand, smiling reassuringly when he saw panic flare in her eyes. 'I'm not leaving you for very long, sweetheart, but I told your father that I'd phone him as soon as you woke up. I'll be straight back once I've spoken to him. That's a promise.'

He kissed her lightly on the lips then hurried away. Natalie closed her eyes as she listened to his footsteps fading. Maybe she was reading too much into what he'd said but she had a feeling that promise hadn't been meant just for the short term.

A smile touched her mouth as she drifted back to sleep because maybe—just maybe—things were going to work out for them after all.

Rafferty finished assuring Richard Palmer that he would phone him immediately if there was any change in Natalie's condition and hung up. Now that the worst seemed to be over, reaction had set in and he felt positively weak with exhaustion as he made his way back to the IC unit. He'd maintained a constant vigil at Natalie's bedside, only leaving her when the staff had forced him to take a break. Fortunately, the consultant in charge of the unit was someone he knew, so he'd been able to call in a few favours, otherwise he wouldn't have been allowed to stay. Now, as he went back to her bed, he could feel his stomach churning with nerves.

He had no idea what was going to happen once she recovered from her ordeal. However, he did know that he was going to carry out that promise he'd made to her. He was going to stay with her for however long she needed him, and when the time came that she could manage on her own, he would step aside. All he wanted was to know that she was safe and happy, and he'd be content.

She was fast asleep when he got back so he sat down and waited for her to wake up. She slept for more than an hour and it was gratifying to see that she looked for him as soon as she woke up, although he couldn't allow himself to read too much into it. In a situation like this she was bound to need the reassurance of a familiar face.

'Back in the land of the living again,' he said lightly, trying not to let that thought intrude. So long as she was safe, that was all that mattered, he reminded himself. 'I've spoken to your father and he sends his love. I managed to persuade him not to rush back here so he'll be in to see you later on this afternoon.'

'Good,' she croaked. 'Don…wan'…him making hi'self ill again.'

'We certainly don't.' He gave her hand a gentle squeeze then went to pick up the beaker of water so he could give her a drink, only she wouldn't let him go. Her fingers clutched his in a surprisingly strong grip.

'There's something I have to tell you, Rafferty.'

Rafferty felt a spasm of terror run through him. There was only one thing he could think of that she would need to tell him so urgently and that was that she didn't want him getting the wrong idea about their relationship. He wasn't sure if he was up to hearing it at that moment, despite his high ideals, so he hurriedly tried to intervene.

'Shh, now. You mustn't keep straining your throat…'

'I…love…you…'

They both spoke together then both stopped. Rafferty heard his own throat rasp this time as he swallowed. He knew that she was waiting for him to say something but he couldn't seem to force a solitary word out of his mouth.

'This is the part where you're supposed to answer.'

Her voiced sounded a little stronger but maybe it was his hearing which had become so acute all of a sudden. Rafferty tried again to make his body obey him but when he opened his mouth a big fat nothing came out. He wanted to tell her that he loved her, too—adored her!—but all he could manage was silence, and it obviously wasn't the response she'd been hoping for.

He groaned when he saw tears start to trickle down her cheeks because he couldn't bear to know that he'd hurt her when she'd just offered him the world on a plate. And it was that thought which finally galvanised him into action.

He took hold of her hand and gripped it tightly with his. 'I love you, too, Natalie, with all my heart and every scrap of my being. I love you so much that I *ache* when I'm not with you. I can't bear the thought of facing the future without you, but I'd let you go in an instant if I thought it would make you happy.'

'I don't want you to let me go,' she said huskily as her tears gathered momentum. 'I want you to hold onto me because I need you…'

She broke off, overwhelmed by both the effort of talking and the emotion of the moment, but he didn't need to hear anything else. She'd told him more than enough, had completely dispersed the cloud that had been hovering over him so that his world suddenly seemed to be lit by sunshine.

Gathering her into his arms, he hugged her to him then cursed roundly when the monitors cheeped out a warning about him invading their territory. Natalie laughed and the sound was like music playing inside his head, so pure and so beautiful that he couldn't think of a more wonderful accompaniment as he kissed gently her on the mouth. He drew back and smiled at her with a wealth of tenderness in his eyes.

'I think we'd better leave the rest until later, don't you?

When you're not wired up to all those machines. I think they're a bit jealous!'

'And so they should be!' She smiled back at him as he pressed a kiss into her palm. 'We're not...behaving very... well, are we?'

'You might not be, but I've been a model of restraint so far,' he contradicted her loftily. He touched a finger to her lips and chuckled when she gasped in outrage. 'Now, now, no arguing. You're supposed to be resting your throat, don't forget.'

She gave a little moue of disgust but obediently settled back against the pillows. 'Then...the sooner I'm out of here the better—that's all I can say.'

'Amen to that,' he replied, kissing her again. 'Amen!'

Two weeks later

'I can manage now. Thank you.'

Natalie straightened up after Rafferty finished helping her out of the car. After the days she'd spent lying in that hospital bed, it felt wonderful to be mobile again. Although she was still rather weak after her ordeal, she was feeling much better. But then it was hardly surprising in the circumstances, was it?

A smile lit her eyes as she watched him walk around the car. He'd kept his promise and spent every possible minute with her these past two weeks. He'd only left her to grab a few hours' sleep when she'd insisted, but more often than not if she'd woken during the night she'd found him sitting beside her bed. By tacit consent they hadn't discussed what had gone on in Honduras but she was no longer worried that they wouldn't be able to resolve their problems. The past two weeks had brought them closer than they'd ever been and talking about their feelings would no longer be the difficult task it had been in the past.

'Think you can make it up the steps or do you want me to carry you?'

Rafferty slid his arm around her waist as he helped her across the pavement. They'd decided to return to Natalie's house for no other reason than that all her clothes were there. She'd have been just as happy to go back to his flat but simple logistics had made it the easier option. Now she grinned as she handed him her keys.

'I should be able to manage the steps if you could deal with the alarm. I don't fancy a repeat of what happened the last time you were here, do you?'

'I most certainly don't,' he snorted, dropping a kiss onto her upturned face in loving punishment for the trick she'd played on him. 'Being hustled into the back of a van by a couple of burly security guards wasn't on my agenda this afternoon.'

'Really?' She batted her eyelashes at him. 'Then may I enquire what *was* on your agenda?'

'Not what you obviously have in mind,' he retorted, ignoring her assurance that she could manage as he helped her up the steps. 'You're supposed to be convalescing, don't forget.'

'How could I forget when you're obviously going to remind me every opportunity you get?' She pouted. 'You have a very cruel streak at times, Rafferty. Has nobody told you that?'

'Hundreds of people.' He dropped another kiss on her mouth and grinned at her. 'But I told them the same thing I'm telling you: it's for your own good. You won't get round me—no matter what devious methods you employ!'

He unlocked the door, ignoring her tut of displeasure at not getting her own way as he deactivated the alarm. Once that was done, he led her straight to the sitting room and got her settled on the couch.

'Right. I'm going to make you a drink so what do you want? Tea or coffee?'

'Neither. I don't need a drink but I do need you.' She held out her hand, watching the rapid play of emotions that crossed his face as he tried to stick to his principles and behave sensibly. 'Come on, Rafferty, you know you want to,' she coaxed.

'I do. Too much!' he admitted with a groan as he sat down beside her.

Natalie sighed with pleasure as she snuggled up against him, savouring the fact that at last they were alone. 'I feel fine, so there's no need to worry. And I promise on my honour that I'll be sensible and not do anything too taxing.'

'I'll hold you to that,' he told her gruffly, putting his arms around her while he nuzzled her hair.

'Mmm, that feels nice,' she whispered, lifting her face for his kiss. The kiss must have lasted longer than he'd intended it to because he groaned when he let her go.

'It's just so hard to behave sensibly when I'm holding you like this, my darling. I want you too much.'

'And I want you, too, just as much.' She turned towards him, cradling his face between her hands. 'I love you, Michael James Rafferty. I always have and I always will. I'm not sure what went wrong when we were away, but I think that you misunderstood what I was trying to tell you. Your background doesn't make a scrap of difference to me. It never has. I love you for who you are and I don't care about anything else. I just want us to be together and spend our lives making each other happy.'

'That's what I want as well. But are you sure I can make you happy? I know you believe that my background doesn't matter, but I couldn't bear to think that one day you might regret being with me.'

'Why should I regret it?' she demanded. 'You're everything I've ever wanted. You're intelligent, handsome, sexy…'

'Oh, so you think I'm sexy, do you?' he growled, leering at her, and she giggled.

'Mmm, I do. Although I doubt I'm the only woman to tell you that.'

'You're the only one that matters,' he said softly, and she shivered when she heard the emotion in his voice.

Leaning forward, she kissed him on the mouth, feeling his immediate response with a rush of pleasure. She twined her arms around his neck and drew his head down so she could deepen the kiss, gasping when she felt his tongue slide between her lips and tangle with hers. When his hand found her breast and began to gently stroke her hardening nipple she cried out and felt him suddenly go still. He drew back and she could hear the struggle he was having to regain control in the roughened timbre of his voice.

'We were supposed to be behaving sensibly.'

'We are. Loving you is the best medicine in the world, Rafferty. It makes all the bad times seem meaningless and puts everything that has happened into perspective.' She pressed her fingers to his lips, shivered when she felt his tongue touch her skin because it was so erotic to feel its warmth there and know that soon she would feel it on other, more sensitive parts of her body. 'I want you, my darling, and I don't care if it's going against all that sensible advice I was given at the hospital because I know in my heart that it's what I need to help me heal.'

'I want you, too, my love…so much…'

The words faded into silence as his mouth found hers again. Natalie kissed him back, showing him through her actions that she'd been telling him the truth. Loving Rafferty and being loved by him was the best medicine in the world for her.

He swept her up into his arms and carried her out of the

sitting room and up the stairs. The curtains were drawn across her bedroom window and they didn't bother opening them because there was enough light to see by as he laid her down on the huge old bed. Natalie didn't say a word as she lay there and watched while he stripped off his clothes then just as quickly rid her of hers. They didn't need words to put the seal on their love—just actions.

Rafferty lay down beside her and his eyes were full of tenderness as he studied the reddened scar left by her recent surgery. It had healed well and she knew that it would fade in time but she didn't feel embarrassed about him looking at it. A scar wouldn't change how he felt about her, just as it wouldn't have changed how she felt about him. Their love was too deep to be affected by external forces.

'I love you, Natalie,' he said softly as he turned to face her, and she smiled at him.

'And I love you, too.'

'I've made a lot of mistakes but the one thing I want you to remember is that I never meant to hurt you. Everything I did, I did out of love for you.'

'I know. And you weren't the only one to make mistakes. We were both at fault, both too stubborn to admit that we had a problem and that we needed to resolve it.'

She kissed his jaw, felt the tremor that passed through him and smiled a secret little smile, because in one respect nothing had changed—his desire for her was just as strong as it had always been, just as strong as her desire for him.

The thought made her shudder and she felt his hand move down her body as he soothed her, yet the caress did little to ease the tension that was building inside her. When he kissed her throat she murmured in pleasure, encouraging him to continue—and he did. His mouth moved from her throat to her collar-bone, his lips skimming along the delicate bones, leaving behind a trail of fire, and the tension increased all the more.

'Are you sure you feel all right?' he whispered, drawing back just enough so that he could study her face.

'Fine. Never better, in fact.'

He laughed huskily so that goose-bumps suddenly broke out all over her body because it was the most deliciously sexy laugh she'd ever heard. 'Good. Then I'll carry on.'

His mouth moved from her collar-bone to the upper swell of her breasts, so tantalising as it followed the slope that led to her right nipple which was blatantly awaiting its arrival. He drew her nipple into his mouth and she cried out when needles of pleasure shot through her as he suckled her, forerunners of all the pleasure that was still to come.

His mouth moved on to her left breast where he repeated the process, and she gasped. With each movement of his tongue her passion was building and it was high time that she repaid the favour. Her hands slid down between them and she felt him stiffen when she began to stroke him intimately, his body quickening with the gentle rhythm until she could feel him pulsing against her, so hard and strong and vital that she couldn't wait any longer. Her hands curved around his back as she urged him to her, but he resisted, shaking his head when she stared at him in surprise.

'No. I don't want to risk crushing you,' he murmured, his hands cradling her face while he dropped kisses on her cheeks, her nose, her jaw.

Natalie was about to protest that she could stand being crushed but couldn't stand not making love to him when he suddenly rolled over, taking her with him so that she found herself lying on top of him.

'That's better,' he whispered. 'There's no danger of you being hurt now, is there?'

Natalie didn't reply—she couldn't because the tension that had been building inside her was fast reaching a peak. When Rafferty entered her in one long, slow thrust she gasped then everything seemed to go wild, colours pulsing and shimmering behind her eyes, her blood pounding inside her, her cries mingling with his. It took her a long time to come back down to earth after reaching such heights and when she did, she could tell that he'd been just as moved by their love-making as she'd been.

'I love you,' she told him with a catch in her voice, because in all the time she'd known him he'd never let her see him so vulnerable before.

'And I love you, more than I've ever loved anyone in my life. You're my whole world, Natalie. I'd be nothing without you, just an empty shell.'

Tears filled her eyes when she heard that confession and she kissed him. 'I'll never leave you again. No matter what happens from this point on, we shall be together.'

'We shall. I don't care what we have to do to make our marriage work but we'll do it.'

'Marriage?' she repeated in utter shock, and he grimaced.

'Yes, marriage. If you'll have me, of course.'

He looked so unsure all of a sudden that she didn't have the heart to make him wait for her reply. Maybe it wasn't the most romantic proposal that had ever been made, but that didn't matter. There was only one man she'd ever wanted to propose to her and he just had!

She kissed him on the mouth then smiled at him with all the love she felt for him clear to see in her eyes. 'I'll have you, Michael James Rafferty. I'll have to, because I can't imagine anyone else putting up with you!'

'Oh, can't you indeed?' He pulled her down to him, kissing her long and hungrily so that she was breathless when he let her go. 'And that's your only reason, is it? Because you've taken pity on me?'

'No,' she replied dreamily. 'It's not the only reason but it will have to suffice for now because when you kiss me like that I can't think straight!'

He chuckled, a definite smugness in his voice as he cradled

her in his arms. 'You're excused from having to answer any more questions in that case.'

'Mmm,' she murmured, because there really wasn't any need to say anything else. She was going to marry this man who made her feel as though she was on her head instead of her heels half the time and they were going to live happily ever afterwards. Frankly, that was the only thing that mattered!

1105/059/MB146